# SCISSORS, PAPER, STONE

a novel by Marcus Boggs

**FRANKLIN WATTS**
*New York / London / Toronto / Sydney*
1981

Excerpt from
"Esthétique du Mal" from
THE COLLECTED POEMS
OF WALLACE STEVENS,
by Wallace Stevens.
Copyright 1947
by Wallace Stevens.
Reprinted by permmission of
Alfred A. Knopf, Inc.

Library of Congress Cataloging in Publication Data

Boggs, Marcus
Scissors, paper, stone.

I. Title.
PS3552.0438S27      813'.54      81-7536
ISBN 0-531-09860-5      AACR2

*For*
*Tom and Philip*

*Lear's Shadow.*

*...How cold the vacancy*
*When the phantoms are gone and the shaken realist*
*First sees reality. The mortal no*
*Has its emptiness and tragic expirations.*
*The tragedy, however, may have begun,*
*Again, in the imagination's new beginning,*
*In the yes of the realist spoken because he must*
*Say yes, spoken because under every no*
*Lay a passion for yes that had never been broken.*

Wallace Stevens

# 1

"Sing me a song, my darling."

She sings like the fountain in the court of the lions, songs of love, hymns of adulation.

"No, my darling, hush. They'll hear you."

But I can feel her smile in the dark. She loves the sound of her own voice and that it pleases me as she loves the touch of her skin and that it pleases me: my sybarite, my cinnamon. Gently, unobtrusively, I implore: reason not the need, measure not the loss.

"You said they can't hear. They've never heard before."

Her muted laughter: the sound of falling water. Buddhist priests are said to seek out glades with waterfalls because the dulcet repetitive sound aids their contemplation. She is my glade, her voice my falling water. But I'm no priest and feel no need for contemplation. No. Here is the end of contemplation: world within the world, diamond implicit in the lump of coal, the statue in the stone. Here no dragon sleeps, no ambiguity prevails. Here everything's as limpid, as fundamental as falling water. World within the world. The tarn of sapphire blue and the sunlight breaking through the foliage which overhangs the pool and my body and the body of my friend Bill the lepidopterist stretched out to dry on a rock above the pool, and the falling water, falling inexorably and rushing thence on to the sea. World within the world. The cooling vapor of a city fountain upon my face and the insatiable sound of falling water which absorbs the harsh abrasive sounds of buses and disputatious voices. The naiads, the ondines, the river gods in round and bas-relief. The eternally innocent, denied experience. Little any longer to my surprise, she has read my thoughts and, smiling in the dark, she commands me,

"Tell me again what we'll do."

"What we'll do when, my flower?" I ask patiently, athirst for the sound of her voice. When: the places I have visited, the fields where I have laid me down to sleep, the ages of my dreams, my banished self. What other time, what other place compares to this. This time, this place: I've never been so happy: pool and falling water. Never lived so with abandon nor felt myself so perfectly contained. The merging of all things to one inestimable thing. My spathe, my flower. She winds her legs around me and I lift her and hold her to my breast and stand by the window. I am a sturdy plant, unaltered through millennia, the traces of which one finds suspended in the dried mud of ancient creekbeds, and she, she is my flower, the labor of millennia, the patient maddening experiment, my flower. I lift and hold her by the window and she thrives in moonlight, my flower of darkness. My flower of flowers. She says,

"When we go to New York, of course."

I sift and sort the images of my wanderings: city more than city, city of cities, city of darkness. The Rock. The Web. So many flies, so many plastic replicas of Prometheus. Rocking, rolling. Rolling with the punches. I tease her,

"What everyone does there: eat too much, drink too much."

"Will we love too much?" She makes her voice intone concern.

"No," I reassure her, "that's one thing no one does too much of in New York."

"Good," she sighs, subsiding. "I would hate to think I might love you too much ever. I'm ready for anything else."

She pauses, then accuses, "You're laughing at me."

Yes, I do not say. Her brave words amuse me. But why not after all. She has never failed herself before and will not be bound by the failures of others nor made to atone for them. So why then not. It is her right to yearn for a wider world, another world, than this: the South, abused, abusing, the suppurating wound: the piedmont in its seasons, its rotations on a point: the red soil, the pale blue line of mountains, the cicadas, the languid leafiness and the still dry heat of summer, the winter twilights, the azaleas. But equally those things to condemn: those infernals, inspiring both horror and pity, tho mostly horror: those blind cave-bound fish. The passionate complacency of fish. The piety: the eagerly reborn: the gasps, the gospels, the hymns, the hems and haws. The risible defense of an indefensible dishonor: two drunken fathers fighting in the parking lot at the debutante ball over who called whose daughter a whore. The horror. Hers the right, the inalienable right to know more than was given her to know, to see things as they are and not as this close perspective makes them seem, or so she says or so she thinks and tries to say. I felt that way once, left for good reason and returned for no reason but the constant aggravation it would cause me, returned, the ironical son, to find in time the world within the world. My spathe, my flower. My happiness constricts my throat. But why not after all. Instead I say to her,

"Ah. Ah. Ah. I love you."

And she nestles her head more securely against my shoulder.

She finds it so easy to be pleased. Drawing breath itself delights her. She has some gift of life, a genius for the mundane. She acts sincerely as if she believes the homilies, eating right, loving one's neighbor, brushing one's teeth, I don't know, bound in that gold-bound book they gave her for perfect attendance through twelve years of Sunday School, the art of living, that icon she keeps on her bedside table and devotedly wears down the edges of, in odd company with the Nietzsche I gave her, which she carefully, slowly puts away like a reluctant but dutiful child eating her spinach. I have never mentioned a subject in which she would not take an interest, troubling her unscarred brow like a wind a lake at evening, some part of which she did not try to understand. I was first amused by her ignorance, that anyone should not know this or that, the obvious, the common currency, that anyone should have failed to profit by the uncertain progress of the mind. But evolution, it is said, does not traffic in acquired characteristics. And I came easily, remembering my own struggle and the embarrassment of my own unknowing, to admire instead her eagerness, her tenacity, her hardiness. She is my flower of the rocks. She adorns the rugged mountains, the mountains of the moon, the desert, wherever there is need of her. A boon to all mankind, her familiar spirits gathered round her, the living rocks erected in the form of a pyramid. She sighs,

"I will always love you, Loren, whatever happens. You are so good to me."

Again I am amazed by the way my word, my living word, distracts her. What could happen. We have talked of it. Whatever. But this is not the time or place, my spathe. Here we are safe, no longer children frightened by the demons the darkness makes of a heap of clothes thrown haphazardly across a chair. Our hearts race to a different urging. She will be silent now and take the measure of my heart. Idly my hand strokes her back, like a series of little waves breaking serenely on a white beach. Her back, the smooth cool comforting drumlike expanse, I know to be hers and my hand, the moon's minion, mine. But after that the distinctions begin to blur. Our hearts beat in echo of each other. Our sighs are vapors of the same deep source. Our hair mingles, entangles, holding us like a web: some preternatural belief. Where my breast ends and hers begins I cannot say. We begin to seem one breast. She often says so much: we are one person: an Indian saying, she says. You possess me, she says. And I have let her say it tho I can no more be said to possess her than an audience can be said to possess a performance. She has had her audience, does not deny it, would not deny it, since still she's at that age when her innocence might be renewed by wanting it. She will not be thought ill of, however much she might profess as well her wish that I had stepped into her life before this, that we might have been together always, O. I know this, know this all, her innocence, her experience. It's Margaret we mourn for. Women have no gift for reticence; I've never known a woman who was not eager to impart her most private thoughts, the details of her previous affairs. None of your goddam business. They know there's power in confession: you make your confidant your slave. So Rousseau knew and so he enslaved his world, a race of chimeras, women's hearts in men's bodies, slaves to themselves, confessing all. Rousseau, trousseau. What moves us to embrace the women whom we choose. The appeal to, the replication of our secret selves, our unsuspected selves. Ah yes: perhaps her innocence however gained is better than this funereal disease I'm marked with. Knowing all and still choosing, yes. I cannot deny myself. Knowing and still choosing. The necessary illusion of our being first in the garden, Adam in Odden, dissipates. Some poor quivering troglodyte was there before us, some fire worshiper who pressed his hand to the wall of the cave and marked it indelibly. Haeckel's law: Ontogeny recapitulates phylogeny. One poor dumb fool and then another moved by want, this pleasure, this release from pain. No. She is not, could not be mine, all mine, as she asserts: too much of herself resides in other men's hearts, herself which she has freely given. Nor am I hers, as she implores. But something there is or isn't between us. We have not shed our sins like skins but seen through them, the Emperor's new clothes. No matter this, it matters all. She will save me yet. My great redeemer cometh. Blasphemer. I have never felt this intimacy before, this, what the hell, this oneness. She merits more than to be loved. One can love so well in haste. My hand continues to break and run serenely on her back. She sighs,

"I wish you never had to leave."

Leave, leaving, unleaving, unloving, loving. Margaret. I tease her.

"That would be a shock, don't you think. My yawning my way down to breakfast unannounced in day-old underwear."

The evoked image amuses her: she shakes with laughter, her head burrowed in the pillow to muffle the sound. It amuses me too, like her in love and so so easily moved to laughter. I begin to sputter, clamp my lips to keep the loud good spirits from running free for anyone to claim, from giving us away. They are nice people, her parents, the salt of the earth, but incapable of dealing with a license so casually acknowledged. My mother, on the other hand, would not raise a hair of her fine eyebrow, would note only that she required clean linen at the breakfast table. She is a woman of immense will and able thereby to smooth the hard edges of the world instantaneously. I don't think I've ever surprised her by some rash act which surprised the hell out of me. Nor for that matter has anyone else, I don't think, except perhaps my father. Nothing else has been too big to get down. She simply will not permit being fooled, the world being what it is, she says, and difficult enough to live in even with the certain knowledge of what is going to happen next. In some ways I can't help admiring her for that. Of what she is she is the nearly flawless being: an existential achievement: one of a kind and that the work of her own hand. She's always been a difficult woman to love, however easy to live with. Given that I suppose I should see the significance of laying myself out with a girl for the first time in my parents' bed, by that time her bed alone: an act of rebellion, sacrilege: pissing on the altar or some such thing. I prefer to think it the most convenient spot for the final loss of that innocence I had been paying out in smaller pieces for years. How long ago was that all. Poor Dick Savage, with nothing to talk about. That slender willing girl, made beautiful by her willingness, that weekend when my mother and sister went away and she told her parents, or didn't tell them, whatever girls do, or they simply didn't care or trusted her and didn't question that the twenty-seven miles was too far to drive home after a party and his mother, my mother, has been nice enough to invite me, her, to stay over so I'll be home Sunday. So there we were, pissing on the altar, at least I was or wasn't, and thinking myself irrevocably in love. And only the next summer, as we drove to the beach, five of us, our graduation from high school just behind us, did it gradually become known and then perfectly in a great tumble of laughing shouting confession that during that same year that same dear thing had revealed the mystery to four of us. And only Dick with nothing to say and now he tells me they're working on their third child and hoping for a son to go with their two daughters. Oh the laughter, the mystery, the fear, the posturing, the clever disobedience. Enthralled to love, in love with love. So much. And yet so ill-prepared. For this. The difference. The difference. I dispel the spirits. I ask, whispering,

"Have they decided then that you are going?"

"Who?" she asks, raising her head. My heart, my heart. To hear just one word from her lips: that joy.

"The powers that be. Whoever told you in the first place that you might go to New York."

"Oh," she says. "Well, it's still not official. But Noel says it's very likely."

The repetitive measure of my hand upon her back, the ceaseless timeless rolling in and rolling out, the long smooth undulations, infinitely gentle; and then I notice that my hand has stopped and my mind alone has continued its caress. The infiniteness of these repetitions enchants me: have true loves ever not found joy

in moonlight and the movement of the sea. This timeless beauty, infinitely repeated. Noel's constancy. Himself as unchanging as the moon. The silver fox. Such
dread seriousness, prying loose those women from
their virtue. My surreptitious comrade in love's initiation with poor Dick's wife before she became his wife.
The timelessness of love and lubricity. The time:
twelve-thirty-seven: the red digits like the eyes of the
elders watching, watching Susannah. The radio clock
I gave her. The disapproving watch of time: on to more
serious matters than love's joy, love's frolic. What.
Blink: twelve-thirty-eight. Is it time. Not yet. My time.
My wild mountain thyme. I opine,

"That sounds like Noel: everything still deferred. Are
he and Celia—"

She interrupts, gasps, giggles softly, "Oh yes. Didn't
I tell you? Timmy caught them at it when he was rum-
maging around looking for something for his windows.
He said it nearly cracked him up. Celia all practical
had just hiked her skirt up around her waist. But Noel
had taken off his coat and pants and folded them as
neat as they are on display."

The image she evokes revokes a memory. The extended stay in Paris: the bedouin's reluctance to leave
the oasis. The Seine, before dawn, an hour when only
the stiffs and the heavyweights are awake. The shrill
call for help as the young woman, unable to swim, was
swept down river. My stumbling unsteadily downstairs
in my pajamas, blanket in hand; the confusion, the
relief to find her rescuer already drawing her to the

quay against the current. The stretched hands from the bank. And then the incongruous detail: the man had taken time, as her life was being swept away, to disrobe to his shorts and then to fold his clothes neatly and stack them neatly on top of his shoes set side by side with military precision. I never learned how she came to be in the river, whether by accident or intent which she instantly regretted, nor how a man could show such coolness at such a time. It is the vision of a moment, the flash of color churned up in the constant restless activity of mind. She adds carefully,

"I don't know what she sees in him. At least she's not so creepy, you know. All that gray hair and all at his age."

"He's just my age. We more or less grew up together."

"Has he always been like this?"

I laugh softly. "Well, he's always known what took priority in his life, if that's what you mean. It must have been rather a strange sight for Timmy."

She begins, then breaks off, giggling. "Now, Loren, be nice. But he did say he had no regrets."

I muse absently. "I'm sure there are a good many women with regrets. He's a good-looking man."

"Oh I know. They can't figure us out at the store, whether he is one like they think or whether we have something going."

"I suppose the arrangement serves him pretty well. You'll keep the Klan off his scent at least. Now that the blacks have gotten so strong, they're looking for someone weaker to persecute. Tell him he'd better watch his step."

She raises her head to look at me in the dark. "Oh Loren, don't be cruel. Timmy's the sweetest man I know."

I defend myself, laughing. "Now wait a minute, wait a minute. I didn't say anything about my own feelings. I was just offering a little advice. He should be grateful. People pay me a lot for my advice. I'm giving it to him for free."

She continues her accusation: "Yes, but I know what you were thinking. You were feeling sorry for him."

I laugh softly with a purpose and begin again to break and run my hand along her back. "No no, I don't have the pity to spare for Timmy. He's made his own choice in the matter, whatever urged him to it. Or I don't feel any sorrier for him than for anyone else who is not me with you. Knowing you, I'd die, I think, to be denied you."

She flutters in the gentle web I've spun, sighs before I close her mouth with my tongue. "Oh Loren."

So to one neutral thing: she presently repeats, in a voice made husky by her passion, "Oh Loren, I love you so." And then is silent.

No more, no more than this, confronted by the inert world, the triumphant beast, who does not share our sufferings or joys: the eternal reverberation, the echo in the hollow of a spoon. And yet something must be said, to turn us from the dull pitiless ignorance of the world. Oh Loren, I love you so. Something: in truth, in earnest, in utter falsehood, I doubt that it matters which, so long as it breaks the still surface of the pond into which we gaze. Something: the rest is silence, tho blandishments may herald it and then dissolve like the fog in morning. The act of love, the celebration of death: primordial things: to speak during either is an insult to the participants. But the first few words afterward mark our momentary triumph over both. I know this and yet remain silent for several minutes, savoring the taste of her which lingers in my mouth, the smooth sweet acidic taste of melon touched with lime, and refusing to part with it so great has been the pleasure, tho ineluctably it begins to ebb and my mouth withers and grows numb. I lie still and absorb the last smell of heat in the ashes, the dying heat upon the hearth, and the various peculiar medicinal odors of our various emissions and exudations, the healing balms. Her flesh has softened and I know she sleeps. Or only slumbers, for when at last I answer her with my own familiar litany, in a broken husky voice, she sighs and draws closer and covers me, against the terrors of the night, with a delicate arm and leg as smooth and priceless as old ivory. I amaze myself: those words, that hollow little echo: how it pleases her, how it pleases me. A blessing to give and to receive. What: what to give. Just me. She does not question what, but loves and trusts to love whatever its poor representation, whatever her deserts. She does not question her goodness. Such peace, such pleasure at the end of pain. And for me this restless activity, the sleepless nights. The shark which never sleeps. I must. In her the agent of my evolution. Drag myself from the sea: the smooth white beach, the tropical paradise, the world within the world. Oh Linda.

"I love you."

She stirs again as the words escape me. I had not meant to speak them, only to rattle them around in my head, like a child shaking a Christmas package in the attempt to discover what it contains. What is that sound: love. I amaze myself. The lie given to my disability and their unworthiness: she merits more than to be loved merely. And me. I learn. The mind's plasticity. Learn anything; learn love. Mind over matter: a heaven of hell, silk purse of a sow's ear. Haven't I all, all but mastered my affliction, my stuttering, my mind at war with itself. When was the last time. Ah yes, of course: when else. The Littlejohns' party last summer when Susan, a little drunk and very loose, insisted that I dance with her. How forget that: that vivid inference of the prey. It gives you a love of language for it to desert you like that; it becomes an addiction, an obsession. Not to speak all the time but just to be able to, without fear that the words will fail to form and leave you embarrassed and panting like a man in pain. It all becomes so precious when it can be denied you by caprice. The limitless possibilities, the intricate convolutions: such a splendid instrument. And more than that, the beauty and the craftsmanship, the impossibility of thought without it and, from that, my fear, that one's thought becomes impoverished as the use diminishes. An autistic child, subsiding, sinking deeper into himself, until he is gone forever, from the frustrations of not having a language adequate to express his thoughts. The failure of metaphor: language of primitives and children. No longer a means of identification but of hiding one's thought, creating ambiguity. Here no ambiguity—

"Stanley."

She stirs, crouches. I comfort her, kiss her brow. In sleep she confronts her demons.

"No."

Amazed I soothe her,

"Shhhh."

Our minds in touch. Reading each other's thoughts. Her brother, my sister. Stanley, her antithesis and thus, I wonder, my equal, *mon semblable, mon frère.* So he thinks at least. An odd equation that: two things not equal to the same thing, equal to each other: guilt innocence experience. A problem in triangulation. Finding one's way. Trinity. Three in one. Hole in one. Whole in one. Purgation, lustration. Innocence *retrouvée.* This mad pursuit of innocence. The green and pleasant land: would Ross Adcock have any idea what I was talking about if I told him his golf course is integral to the American dream as dreamt in our time: the last elusive frontier, *ce recoin.* The national pastime. Last haunt of the rugged individual. It is living art, the satisfying illusion, the entirely useless enterprise charged with meaning and importance, the release from strain, the terrible wearing of the mundane and insoluble, by the creation of another tension and the release from it. I suppose I do like the stakes after all, the few bills changing hands at the end of the round, but that is no more than the child's ascription of value, entirely arbitrary. There are so many things to love about the game without it: the order and pattern of formal gestures, the solitude, the splendid setting as seductive and ominous as a Greek isle, the intellection required. That especially. So many things there are to go wrong, so much attention to be paid, so accurate the translation of mental activity into physical activity. The perfect swing: hands, feet, knees, hips, shoulders, elbows, head at rest when addressing the ball; the backswing, swing, follow-through. At times I think I concentrate so much on those that I lose all consciousness of the ball. I can remember it afterward only as a momentary interruption of the swing and a distant hollow sound. That time Nicklaus lost his hat in the wind as he stood over a putt: he didn't know it, even after the ball had dropped; his caddy had to retrieve it. The intellection then. Powers of mind directed to the solution of a problem, the conspiracy of mind and muscle against the hazards of the environment—ponds, creeks, the encroaching wood, sand traps. Ah the word, the hollow sound. The images convoke like vultures. The memories. Twenty-five years ago. So tenacious the mind's hold. What we regret. What we cannot refuse. There's not a trap I've been in which has not called Billy Roddy to mind, his face suddenly a red mask, his gaping mouth, tragic and comic simultaneously. His screams, more in fear than pain, I expect, and yet he still sports the scar my pail impressed on his forehead and when drunk calls everyone's attention to it and once wanted to fight about it, to get even after all these years. Now just hold it, Billy: your mother got even on the spot.

You little monster, she called me. I was. Am. What moved me to it. Some things don't bear remembering. The freudian couch a procrustean bed. Make me like other men: stretched, cut down to size, well adjusted. The detestable self already all too human. The horror. Billy Roddy and his first mask. What moved me to it. Whence. The genetic endowment: chromosomal anomaly: monster indeed. Some great crime. I will never marry. The horror.

"No."

She sleeps still, the sleep of the just. Her thoughts can follow mine so far, no farther. Such ease: what is is, what will be will be. Our little lady of the earth. Cornucopia. Realms of gold. Your great diviner cometh. Miner: grave robber. Grave maker. What. Whence. Something out of nothing. Spontaneous combustion. Brain on fire. *Cerveau plein de feu.* Nightmare when still awake. Must sleep. Work. That must be it. The nightmare from which I am trying to awake. All too human. The manifold horror. Unfolding and unfolding. Mille-feuille. Millville. Mudville. Just recently, leaving Nashville, Westmoreland in the waiting room of the airport. The pleasant surprise of perception: the famous face made familiar by the newspapers and TV. Then the recognition: the executor of those horrors, that communal madness. Then, finally, the cognition: the little remorse that face evinced: little, none. An ordinary citizen, a businessman in transit, ravaged only by the cares of profit taking and missed connections and not that he once spent human lives like pennies. What plots he now spins, corrupt and unrepentant. I find myself staring at him, my face as hard as stone. Our eyes meet, then his stray on with consummate lack of interest. If he has thought of me at all, it is to groan inwardly at the next anonymous judgment on him, against all reason: I saw my duty and I did it, my country called, it's just my job, it's not my job. Am I wrong. Does he feel remorse. I pass by close, to verify that it is he, the grainy image on the newsprint. *General of the Army* is embossed on his briefcase. Yes. No. I do not speak. He has heard it all before, and either does not need my reminder of his sins or has never and will never acknowledge them. I save my breath. But then I begin to suspect my motives. Fear. The authoritative figure. I will not bear it. Damn him. But when I return to the waiting room, he has gone. When I tell Linda, she asks who is Westmoreland. Childe William. Awakening from the nightmare. Who. A lesion of the collective hippocampus. We cannot forget. Santayana's law. I tell her. She tells me to leave him alone, suggesting that he has probably suffered enough already. No, we can't forget. She ascribes always the best motives, intentions; will rout evil from the world by denying it. Without knowing it, that I need even to be saved, she saves me. Redeemer and diviner. She will save me unaware, provide my ethical education: forgive, forget; beauty and humane feeling. I've far to go to reach that latter state, state of grace. Forgive, forget: how my other notions have changed. The natural history of taste. A taste for mushrooms and *avocats*. A sure sign of one's getting older, the change in one's taste: never satisfied, always volatile. What is

worthy, what is beautiful, the restless eye of the be-
holder. But the contemplation of beauty is a constant,
a verity. That always: the mark of Cain. What. What
did I once love and hold beautiful. What. The first I
can recall: as a lad, emerging from basketball practice
to winter twilights, my hair under the parti-colored
stocking caps we wore, the school colors, red white
and blue, changed from the ancient purple and gold
the day after FDR declared war on Japan, still wet from
the shower, to see the last soft hues—the grays, the
pinks, the purples—of that day never to be seen again.
That first: at fifteen. That keen awareness that there
was something good and powerful and beautiful in the
universe, but ephemeral or very far away and constantly receding. The storms, the imaginary landscapes:
the low wooded mountains of my youth, the high
snowy mountains of my young manhood; the sun
dropping gracefully like a new penny behind Chios as
we sat on the quay at Cesme and drank wine and
waited for the ferry, the stars falling on the wheatfields
of France, the hurricanes along the Carolina coast, the
mist in Boulogne, the smogless day on Lake Como,
the sunlight flashing among the leaves as we rode south
by train from Munich and the ominous beauty of the
Starnbergersee taking us by surprise: remembered,
reconstructed, loved passionately. But ten or fifteen
years older, I've begun to find a beauty in less dramatic
form: the twisted aleatory beauty of a twig in winter,
the fragile curve of a woman's ear, the bead of water
on a leaf, the truth in a grain of salt. My world has
contracted, it seems. Wait: haven't thought of that in

years. The microscope my father gave me for Christmas when I was twelve. Forgotten all about it. Was this what he meant. Where is the thing. Living in a closet somewhere all these years, I guess. Must look for it. Did my father know beauty and seek by that to inspire a love of beauty. No: wait. I remember. I said telescope and he got it wrong, as he always did. Close but no cigar. No matter. I must look for it. Must be somewhere. Open new world: microcosm: quarks, narcs, nerds, neutrinos, things and antithings. My little world, *Tiergarten*, garden. Tending my own garden. The concentration and selection inevitable with growing older, the pressures of the quotidian, the inability to correct or alter a mind grown used to attention to detail. Perhaps I've just grown domestic from sleeping with the same woman even if secretly all these months. Domestication of the savage beast. Tamed at last. How long. It seems like always. January. The new life: new leaf. Lazarus risen from the tomb. Harold. Must try again to have him join us. An offer he can't refuse. No: when. February, I think. Time and circumstance enough that I missed her at the Masters, Sneed's remarkable collapse under pressure. Fuzzy Wuzzy, was he. No: wait. By then we had not made love. Or had we. It doesn't matter: it could be always. Perhaps it's simply that I've found or made so little time to travel lately, spent so much time on the other hand in conference with my fellow man, shifting their deadweight to my shoulders: Wilson and his problems, Bamberger and his. Maybe it's simply the small beauty itself, the simple joy of watching over weeks the unfurling of a flamelike leaf of the snake plant which sits on my desk, the poor plant my mother never fails to complain about when she comes to my office, calling it a memento from a seedy hotel, like towels or ashtrays from places you would much sooner forget, and hurting its feelings. Whence that joy, measureless by any instrument, a neuroscope. No matter, I suppose. The beauty is enough itself and survives the amusement of my colleagues when they see me with my copper watering can. There are some things I no longer have to know. No: no need to kid myself. If so, then why at the heart of pleasure, in the happiest state I have ever known, remain I so easily distracted, prey to these afflicting memories, images, ideas, words. No. Why can't I sleep if I am satisfied. Sleep as she sleeps, undisturbed and confident and fearless. She will teach me. Arrest, reverse this coming to nothing: ineluctable coming: coming and coming and coming. What answer does one give to an accident. The broken pattern. Our own pattern: the ancient pattern redrawn. Love, time, space inhering in the mind. My mystery: Linda Linda: my enigma. Alexander's ragtime band. Apply the sword to the Gordian knot: so much for that. No. She eludes me still: that tremendous ease of movement, that confidence of place, that simple satisfaction with the things which brush against her. Accepting things without rebellion which she need not accept as if they were natural law and inviolable. Doing things, while humming to herself, which I would ponder on for years. Making no bones about her ambitions, her desires, the course of her life, as if it were the most natural thing in the world that secrets should be shared, as if they would dry and crumble in the dark. And yet contriving never to demean herself. Were one to think ill of her, it would be his loss, not hers. My mother would, I think, and Susan would not think at all, as she never does. What is it that attracts me so. An honesty she takes for granted. An ease with those emotions, the like of which in me have appalled me. I can't claim the beauty in me as she can implicitly. I have not found it yet for all my delving, the inexhaustible vein of precious stones: emeralds, rubies, diamonds, the hard glittering rain through my fingers. Rather, the alchemist stoops over his bench, instead of digging for the treasure, attempting to fabricate it, the only glitter the glint of the flame under the limbeck reflected in his eyes. I have the feeling there is nothing about her that I don't know and, simultaneously, little about me that she does. It seems not to matter, her revelations and my reticence. I wonder what she would do: that is mystery. Her generosity accept my intolerance; her calm diffuse my rage. The attraction of opposites: so facile a law will satisfy me until some revolution brew and break. A child's law to explain the universe, a law which ignores and hence denies conflicting evidence. Or indeed my secret self. No matter. Bad laws are as comforting as good, so long as they are evenly applied. What one learns in law school: paradox: how bad laws are in fact good. But then we all embody our little contradictions: the glib stutterer, the illicit lawyer, the disengaged lover, the gregarious recluse. And she: a woman incapable of deception, forthright, and yet embarked upon a

clandestine affair; a timid pride which tests its wings
and a humility, a recognition of her place in the world
which she does not dispute; a natural dignity, a refusal
to be made light of, and yet the eager self-abasement,
the supination demanded of her sex; her innocence
and yet her native power. When we first met, those
steady pale green eyes and my willing consternation
as I balanced between two shirts I did not want, one
in each hand, as if I could judge their quality by weigh-
ing them in that manner. Stopping suddenly and in-
venting an excuse: shirts. Those eyes, that eager smile:
no deception, she actually believes this. That childlike
doll-like prettiness, but just enough to warrant a second
look, a third, an examination: I'm still not certain that
she will never be beautiful. The buttons of her blouse,
the glimpse of throat, but her breasts so small that she
needn't wear a bra and only does because she started
when it was important for her to and it became a habit
and now continues because it is company policy—sex
but not too much nor too obtrusive. She had been
placed in that department, for the time, for just that
reason: to seduce the customer into buying something
he didn't want or need. So there, a sacrifice to theory,
a goat upon the altar of modern marketing: I bought
the shirts and only discovered later, when I got home,
that they were sixty-five percent polyester, my father's
fiber, and so gave them to Ernest who took them with
that same despondent look he turns on everything. I
did get something from it tho with as little grace, thrown
off my stride by the ambivalence I felt, the raw sexual
attraction for the bright-eyed thing, who might not

know another thing to say than that the shirts wash extremely well, and the suspicion that she was not the kind of woman on whom to vent one's desires at my age, a paper cup no fitter than for ordinary wine, that attitude finding its way into solid form by my impulsive suggestion that it would be easier for me if we met halfway between the buildings where we worked, then yes, the perfect spot, the Greyhound bus station, for reasons I knew almost as soon as I said it. So beautifully apposite, I thought, for one who'd not quite outgrown his well-bred taste for whores, and yet I was ashamed I'd made it even from the moment I did and she, a little puzzled perhaps, accepted it. It was not the evening, but the way she ended it which kept me after her. She insisted, when it was time to take her home, that I drop her at the bus station and leave her there where she could take a cab. She would brook no opposition, she would hear no reason, she would consider no argument. I left her where I found her, having taken first the hand she extended to me and attempted to take the depth of those eyes clouded then with shadows. But then I waited, carefully in her sight, puzzled myself then, delighted, feeling acutely that our positions had been reversed and that she was the one gifted with wit and character, until the cab she called had come. I could not wait, but followed the cab to her home; overtook her as she crossed the tattered lawn, her head down advancing before her like a prow; said how pleasant I had found the evening, how much I had enjoyed her company, the usual dull repetitions until the message condescended to show itself: tomorrow night, I asked. She seemed to close upon herself, and instinctively I grasped her elbow gently. Please. Then yes, she said, recovering her smile, yes. Pick me up at the bus station. The same time. I flushed with shame and she was gone, the echo of her laughter, the faint scent of her perfume gone a bit sour, wrapping around me like a veil. I turned away to find the cab still waiting where it had stopped to let her out, the cabbie apparently concerned that I would do her harm and then, too easily reassured when he saw us part, pulling away. So there. The first maneuver to establish the ambiguous symbiosis: love given, love received. A case for the couch: my own exhaustive search for a woman to merit the intimacy, the indignation brought on by disappointment, and yet the search renewed, the pace redoubled, to end inconceivably in this. I would not have thought. No. So long the need unanswered. No. Was I so little loved as I thought then. The empty house. No: not unloved, but not loved either: the object of some pride to my parents, like one of the Ming vases, and expected to remain so, an unobtrusive beauty. The discharge of their social responsibility: one had children then: that ended the discussion. You are our little emissary. I thought they said missionary and thought of Africa. A little emissary: it sounded bad: expelled from the garden, as if I did not belong, Adam and Eve and Pinchmetight. Have I always felt I did not belong. Anywhere. My wanderings. Did not deserve. Just because price is no object for us, my father used to advise me, on those occasions when I had ransomed my honor with a few dollars from his pocket, like that time I threw a rock through old Miss Mercer's window because we thought her a witch and hated anyone who kept indoors and watched our play from behind chintz curtains and got caught for it, just because there is no price doesn't mean there isn't a cost. Us. People like us. We are what we eat. The raw money. The repugnant irony is how little that satisfies. The greater the satiation, the greater the appetite. The loss of measure, inhibition, all control. By some means the mechanism snaps into action, the cells increase at a maddening rate, the cancer grows. The rich a cancer, myself that rich. But no one talks of it. Money. The disease remains undiagnosed. Instead the talk is of private things: one's sexual exploits: who sleeps with whom or what. The more shocking, the better. It's Margaret we mourn for. Stonebreaker. Petereater. The modern woman. That poor benighted creature. Creature of the night. Succubus or vampire. Keeping to her coffin by day. Day and night. The inevitable revolutions. That will be next: the assault on sex, like the nineteenth century assault on wealth: property is theft, behind every great fortune is a great crime. Ha, that's it, that explains it. The great crime. The great criminal of that great crime passed along his genes to me. Gee Officer Krupke. I never had a chance. Genetically determined. *Le goût pour l'égout.* The lust for the illicit. Corrupted before I had a chance. Original sin. And what the difference that I never rose above it. Overcoming and overcoming. Joined that haunted handful, the world's great men. Men more than great. Even Newton finds his earthly limitations. The course of history would be unchanged had Shakespeare and Mozart never lived. Auden said something like that, tho their effect is scarcely the point. They made it possible, no more. They could not alter it. History. What history, I say; there is no history without advance. As always: the same vanities, the same hypocrisies, the same meanness of spirit, the same desperate illusions and expediencies, the same raw striving for preeminence at the cost of others, the same contempt. How familiar, after all, and how inevitable. A familiar ring to that. No fundamental change since the first caveman stood erect and exposed his genitals to the elements: hey, look at me, look what I can do with this. What that means: any spiritual change will only follow a structural change. Mutation. Evolution. Man is what he is: no more to be expected of him. The only question whether he will bring about his own evolution, whether the evolution he seems determined to bring about will be advance or retreat. Retreat from mind. Could be no worse. Menace to himself. What other animal destroys its own environment. Sheep. Moths. Rapacious. None with a brain to speak of. None with imagination, anticipation of the future. And yet those gifts have no effect. Destruction of the ozone layer for the dubious benefit of a mountain of plastic meat trays. Inconceivable. The willful creation of a cinder in space so that we can test to the full our ability to adapt to a hostile environment. My God. The moon anticipates the world to come. These sons and daughters of the moon, this race of lunatics, this loathsome pack of rats.

"No."

I must sleep. What. One-thirteen. Restore energies. Find self. Complete the circle. Yin and yang. A broken wheel: kerthump kerthump. That incompleteness. Mistress sister mother. How many women have I known. Run together after a while: develop common features: the distinctive mark I remember, a mole, gets assigned to the wrong breast, no matter how often my tongue drew rings around it. The ineluctable stages of development: attraction, urgency, satiation, boredom, recrimination, remorse, disengagement, emptiness. No sorrow, no tomorrow, except occasionally for myself. That terrible restiveness. Nor have I remained friends with former lovers. Too much lost to them for far far too little gain. We smile at each other stiffly at the country club bar. Civilities. Know too much. The memory too strong. The smell of Mary Ann in heat. Taking each other for machines, planned obsolescence, to be discarded when the proper use had been made. Or was it Mary Beth's smell I remember, fecund rich earthlike, the best thing by far about her. Whoever. This file of hazy memories: one stacked upon the other so that a common outline appears. The psychologist who sought a common physiognomy for criminals by this method. Galton, I believe. Darwin's cousin. I can't remember. Recognize them on the street. My common lover: something about them: the little cells of eye and brain begin to pop, like a frog's when it detects a fly on the wing. Pattern of my tastes. How similar they are even before the action of my mind upon them. But then the anomaly: then how to explain this. She does not fit the pattern: not my type. But Loren, isn't she rather, well, unpresentable, you know what I mean. And Susan with her two cents: oh Mother hush, I think she's rather charming, like one of those little peasant dolls from Yugoslavia or some place like that. And yet me: I've never been so happy. What. What is it. The long drives, at eighty ninety, neither of us expressing interest in the destination we had set and then each admitting it and driving on and on, to Rachmaninoff, passed occasional farmhouses and through small towns, crossroads with blinking yellow lights, the bottle of wine, the few scattered phrases. What now; play it again. Our hermetic floating world. Then out of it and into a truck stop, starving and laughing, for something to eat. The old pattern has been broken, new cells come into play. The new pattern forms, similar but unique. We are not so different, but different enough. Fragile, ephemeral perhaps, but entirely beautiful. Coming together: I wish, I wish. A star. That infinity or this: suspended between the two. Infinity to infinity. Oversoul to oversoul: measureless to man. Suspended. A snowflake: a—

   She stirs, contracts, huddles more securely into her pearly carapace of sleep. I see my chance and slip my arm from under her head and massage it gently until the circulation is restored. The tingling in my arm is like warm champagne. The air in the room is cool and still and refreshes me, but it will not last and I must go. Already she has learned my movements, my intentions, my presences and my absences, better than I know them myself; and she catches me with a broken phrase at the edge of the bed:

"Wha?"

Pleased, amused, happy, I stretch across the narrow bed and whisper, "No, my love. You go back to sleep."

She mumbles, settling down, "You too."

I agree, "Yes, me too. I have to leave. I have to sleep too."

She murmurs: "Yes, no. Don't leave. I sleep better with you here."

I argue, feeling my cheeks grow taut with amusement, with anticipation of what already I know will follow. "You'll sleep fine."

She wakes. "Put your arms around me until I go to sleep again. Just for a few minutes."

Ah yes, ah yes; the words rustle in my throat: "Like this?"

She laughs softly, as soft, as soft, and pushes me gently away. "No darling. Lay back."

I let the solecism pass, my chance to make her over, and comply, surrender, already beginning to feel the wind gather in my throat, the fierce hot wind of Pluto lusting for Proserpine, the doomed man, the hanged man. Her breath plays over me like the breath of spring, carrying to me not the scent of flowers but the odor of raw earth and tumescence. Her lips like little crabs are an exquisitely devised torture and despite myself I groan. Already I sense the pleasure at the heart of pain, the pain of this longing. My hands seek her hair and gently I draw her face to mine. It is time, passed time, time to come, world to come, world without end, world within the world. I bite my lip, her lip, trying to defer the final moment, knowing the final moment to be the final moment, holding myself back, back until I hear above the rush of blood in my ears the answering wind rising. Our breaths meet and set spinning into eternity a host of vortices. We populate a universe with our passion. Our lips have parted. The blackness. The myriad stars. The ebony gate. The black hole. Spasms take me: a rag shaken by a dog. These rags of time. And then. And then.

Light. Fulguration. A flash.

"My God!"

"What?"

A flash. A second flash.

She hisses between her teeth: "My God!"

Her deadweight on me. I struggle. The drowning man. Air.

"What?"

I struggle under her. The manikin breaks free, cold after her warmth. But no more.

A flash. A third flash.

A laugh: low mean nasal.

I struggle with her deadweight on top of me.

I answer her: "My God!"

She moans: "Stanley. Stanley and his camera."

I hiss struggling: "Goddam."

Blackness. A myriad stars.

I hiss, displacing her finally: "I'll kill him. I'll kill the son of a bitch."

She weeps silently.

The house again is dark and still as a tomb.

# 2

The furnishings of the room where they sat, waiting for the others to arrive, showed no failure of taste and, to those who knew such things, the expenditure of a great deal of money. What was equally true but not so readily evident, because they had worn so well, was that the possession of the major pieces—the stately sofa upholstered in a subdued flowery print, the playful love seat framed in walnut, the *fauteuils* in which there appeared to be not one straight line, the richly elegant side table with its Delft vase into which went thrice a week a fresh arrangement of bursting flowers, the console with its brooding bronze Buddha, the little cherrywood desk cleared of everything but a small brass lamp and the day's unopened correspondence, the four Oriental carpets like blooming oases on the pale expanse of deep pile wool which covered the floor—

had been the act of a single day, a day of utter ecstasy thirty-two years before. Only the oils and watercolors, the bibelots in porcelain and crystal, the discreet photographs in oval silver frames had been slower to accumulate; and only by that idiosyncratic collection could one discover any sense of movement or development, any sense that things were not fixed and permanent like the tomb of a pharaoh, a setting fit to be pillaged and for little else. Rather than clutter and disrupt the original design, however, the ornaments played with it, stood in relation to it as the trills and appoggiaturas to the main argument in Baroque music: their absence would have been noticed, that is, tho their presence rarely was. The various pieces, both great and small, stood now in splendid harmony. Nothing was out of place, and no place better left to itself was filled. For that reason, and because there was not a book to be seen, the room had a distinct quality of nature about it, of nature trimmed to human purposes surely, in the manner of a formal garden, but of nature nonetheless. Even those who entered there with no knowledge of Mrs. Owings' skill as a gardener could not fail to be impressed nor to think that what the Lord had intended had by her been accomplished.

That one day thirty-two years ago and eight weeks before she was to become a bride had satisfied Mrs. Owings completely. She never thought seriously thereafter of altering the room; and her husband, until his death after eighteen years of marriage, had always to congratulate himself on that he had kept pretty much to himself, during that period of joyful anticipation, his shock, indeed his outrage, that she had made bold to lay out so much money—all his too, every penny—before the knot had been officially tied. He could easily afford his magnanimity and, in deference to the occasion, had consoled himself that at least now he knew and knowing could act to prevent a repetition of the performance and had contented himself to ask only, presently, whether she had left anything in the store for the next couple setting out to furnish a house. But in that too she was already a good half-dozen paces ahead of him. She had had her way once. That was enough. There was nothing further to acquire nor to prove. She was herself frugal by nature and by training (her family's distress during the thirties had been the genteel kind; they had fallen from grace, to be sure, fallen with the rest; but even so they had striven to maintain the old appearances, and their meals, tho now they consisted of hotdogs and baked beans, had continued to be served them by their old Negro servant in the old ornate silver vessels) and after the initial laying in saw no reason to alter any element of a design she still loved, loved more in fact with years of acquaintance. Vanity was no reason, and the mere desire for change was no reason, and boredom with the same old things was no reason. She was not vain, at least not to excess, at least not in this way, at least not to the point of pitching out the dollar value, at that time, of four sturdy houses and leaving nothing to show for it but the shallow depressions in the carpet; she was seldom bored and took it out in other ways than spending money frivolously (usually in spending it wisely) when she was; she detested change for its own sake and cleaved to the past only a little less passionately than she did to the present (the future she would not regard or would so only with chagrin). When the pieces began to show their wear, she had them refurbished. Only when something new was needed—a suite for her daughter, a new washer-dryer—did she regain that startling form of her young womanhood. But then she had known the worth of her man, had known that tho he might complain—which to his credit he did not—he could easily absorb the expense; and she had taken as given that some special advantage or privilege accrued to her for agreeing to marry an older man, for taking on, that is, that risk. He had not been so much older, for all that; and at the time of his death, it was generally thought that he had yet a good many years left in him. But a great beauty, she had had her pick of young men struggling to get started after the war; and instead, she had chosen the settled and established life, the glass flower he held out to her almost reluctantly (he had been a bachelor for so long) with a hand already a bit pale, a bit tinged with yellow. And if she felt a responsibility to him for giving it to her— everything, every conceivable thing—she felt equally his to her for her surrendering to him her many opportunities. In the bargain, neither felt stuck with the short end of the stick: he had acquired a beautiful devoted wife for, in the long run, according to his abilities, a fairly modest expenditure; she had had assured immediately the life she aspired to and thought even her due at the cost of his possibly taking flight well before she herself was ready to let him go or in the manner of an Indian princess to accompany him. It had helped too, in their separate regards for their fates and fortunes, that in courtship they had fallen sweetly, suitably in love with each other. After his death, however happy she had been in the institution, she never considered remarrying. By that time of course her son was sixteen and at a difficult age to swear allegiance to anything, especially to a new father. And when she no longer had that excuse to avail herself of, the pain of separation had boiled down to lack of interest. It was thought that she simply did not want to risk the pain again. Had she heard that expressed, she would have smiled and let it pass. In her own mind, however, she was certain simply that she would never find his like again and could never do with less. The proposals came of course, three or four a year, then more as she grew older and more of her near contemporaries found themselves also forced suddenly to carry on alone. But none tempted her; and tho she was not above a little flirtation at her age, she subtly made it known very soon to whoever came to call that she fully intended to live out her life with no more family to her credit than her own two children.

Mrs. Owings in age and adversity had yet retained her beauty. She was fifty-six years old, and primarily because her hair was snowy white, she looked the possessor of those years. But her bones were fine and unaltered; her bearing was that demanded of a queen or fashion model, tho in actual height she was more the former than the latter, and different from either she wore under normal conditions an amused tolerant smile, which most people found rather disconcerting by the third or fourth meeting but then eventually learned to ignore—whatever the smile meant they were never likely to find it out. Her pleasures and her habits were the kind to keep her body trim and her spirits young. She did not smoke; she imbibed a moderate number of spirits. She was an avid tennis player, regularly the club champion for her age group. She took pride in her greenhouse and extensive garden and spent many hours in every week tending her flowers, herbs, and vegetables. Rather than have Ernest drive her, she walked the mile and a half to Turner's Grocery (the seed from which had grown over the last thirty years a meandering chain of twenty-one stores stretched throughout the piedmont, that first unassuming establishment which old Mr. Turner kept open as a reminder to his family of their humble origins and as a favor to those old and valued customers who had brought him their business when times were harder and who wanted the old ways, mutatis mutandis, maintained) and then the mile and a half back with her laden wire two-wheeled handcart drawn behind her. Her face, framed in her remarkable white hair, cut short and swept back in the manner of a much younger woman, showed the lines but not the weightiness of her years. Her features were almost those of her wedding portrait: a long straight nose, beginnning just a bit to dip; brown almond-shaped eyes, showing now a slight puffiness at the corners; an inevitable coarsening of those lips which her husband in the first giddiness of his love, devoid of talent tho he was, had tried manfully to bronze in verse, a testament which had made her weep at the time and made her still when, in the privacy of her own room, on his birthday or their anniversary, she removed the worn scrap of blue paper from the felt-lined box where it was kept and ran her fingers and her clouding eyes over the familiar lines.

She was not in general an emotional woman. She had concluded, in the aftermath of her husband's death, that she could not hold up her end of the business if she allowed herself the luxury of her own feelings for very long at a stretch. Thus she confirmed a principle inculcated in childhood. She had her moods surely, her periods of depression and anxiety; but she did her best to curtail them, to bring them to an untimely end. There was too much to be done, too much ground to be gained, to waste one's time in that fruitless labor. At the same time she knew well how the odds could be stacked against one, how nothing, nothing, for years together might go one's way. From those derived an attitude toward the world which much resembled a sense of irony and a policy toward it never to expect too much—of anything: of the circumstances she found herself in, of the abilities of her kind, of the fidelity of her friends, of pure dumb luck—but also always to take boldly and without shame or guilt whatever was duly offered and that to which no one else could establish a prior claim. If on occasion she made sure to encourage and elicit the offer, well, that was simply the way things were in the world and one had always to look out for herself. That policy made her, to the percipient at least, appear somewhat too frequently to calculate, to scheme, to exploit, to take advantage: one could almost read her thoughts: What will my little flourish of anger cost me? But the percipient were few and far between and a good many of them were put off the scent by her robust self-deprecating humor. That she made jokes about herself, called attention in that manner to her human foibles, dimmed their eyes to her subtle but vigorous and nearly constant prosecution of her and her family's cause. If that stratagem failed, if the jokes began to show too much revision, one might then assume that she simply didn't have time and energy enough, after tinkering in the works of the community, abetting the plots of the church, tending her garden, chasing tennis balls, and especially running the mill, as she called it (in fact an archipelago of mills for the manufacture of cloth, which her husband had consigned to her care and which her son refused to have anything to do with), to trouble herself with so trivial a triumph as their social success—her daughter's election as homecoming queen, for example, when that had been a victory worth gaining, and her son's marriage, which she had so far failed to effect. Years before, when the latter subject had first been broached, he had declared only half in jest that, were he to marry, his partner would have to be either a Jew or a Negro and that, if she were still insistent, he would see whom he could find. She had laughed of course; she had had to laugh. But once, in a moment of weakness, she had felt compelled to warn him that marriage was difficult enough already without making it more difficult by joining, as she put it, individuals from different cultures. Her daughter posed just the opposite problem for her: she had apparently simply too many young men from whom she had to choose. But then she was younger than her son, a good bit younger and seemed younger still, so free and openhearted. And it would only be a matter of the time she had to kill before she decided on the right one. No, Susan did not worry her; but her black prince, as she had once named him, did.

This day, however, that problem was as far from her mind as she could place it. Of her other interests, two—the workings of the community and the plottings of the church—found themselves in cooperation; and the two ladies present, she and her friend of longest standing, Mrs. Blankenship, awaited the arrival of officials from both parties. It was afternoon of a splendid day in early October. The season was slowly gaining its stride: the foliage, following the dogwood's lead, was beginning to change but still showed mostly green; the football season was still young enough that its losers might still nurture hopes of a dramatic comeback, to finish at a highly respectable seven and four; that lioness of fashion Bertie Waddell was well into her wearing of the habiliments she had bought during her semiannual descent on New York months before and had therefore ceased the round of calls she made to show them off, preening and pretending an impulse ("Oh I was just driving by and thought I would drop in for a minute, but only for a minute, mind") or the discharge of a gravely neglected obligation ("Oh it's simply been too long since we had time to sit down and chat"), the demands of both of which, impulse and obligation, were answered within no more than twenty minutes. The cidery air was a draught prepared for the fearless and the inexperienced: in the bubbles was a faint taste of winter, but for those who did not dread the change of seasons that depth after the griddlelike heaviness of summer was welcome. No frost yet went in search of pumpkins to anoint, and the cornstalks still stood, tho dying and fading in the sun and giving up slowly like myriad ghosts, in melancholy chorus, a dusty sweet smell. The low staid mountains to the north and west, the first line of the old Appalachian chain, stood out blue and precise as they did in summer only after a heavy rain had settled the heat. It was that time of year which invites an awareness of itself. The memory of summer vacations had begun to fade; the respite from one's labors granted by the long weekend over Thanksgiving was still too far off to anticipate. But the days at that time of year in that place, except for those visited by unexpected catastrophe, were their own reward. And a certain kind of citizen longed throughout the year for just this time.

Three logs burned merrily in the fireplace between the ladies waiting. The fire cast little light and an unnecessary warmth at their feet. But Mrs. Owings always said a fire completes a room, and even in summer, when her moods were upon her, she would have Ernest lay out the logs for her and would sit staring into the lambent flames until the wood was consumed.

When asked about her habit once, she had retorted dreamily that her fires were less expensive than a shrink and less dangerous than Valium. She had liked the retort so much that it became a refrain for her when she felt witty or wished to get the better of an interlocutor; otherwise, she said merely that she liked fires. Mrs. Blankenship liked fires too, and this one she found very much to her taste: a good thinking fire, she called it, and upon entering the room shortly before had insisted that Willie May, the maid (so named by a disappointed father in honor of the great centerfielder), convey her compliments—Mrs. Blankenship's—to Ernest, her husband—Willie May's—on his accomplishment, as one might ask a waiter to convey compliments to a chef. The best things in Mrs. Blankenship's world were those, designated by the gerundive, one could enjoy doing something with—a good thinking fire (not that in which to burn old love letters or canceled checks six years old), a good drinking bourbon (as opposed to that which one served at a cocktail party, given to discharge an obligation), a good fishing stream (the recognition of which she had gained in thirty years of spending her husband's vacations hip deep in the next pool above his). Hers was a sensibility which suffered little nonsense. Things for which beauty was claimed had to be beautiful; things for which utility was claimed had to be useful; things for which it was claimed that they promote rest and relaxation had in fact to do so. She had been extremely dubious that her husband's hobby would do for her (she needed the rest as much as he after putting up with his demands and the world's inanities) what he claimed it did for him, and she had fought him on it right up to the moment when he had taken her by the elbow and escorted her curtly into midstream. Why not Europe, just once? she had implored. I didn't leave anything there when I left, he had said, giving voice to his lingering resentment that he had been drafted for his essential skills at the age of thirty-four; and it's my goddam money. In him she had met her match, tho only reluctantly would she give up the fight, a man of rare pertinacity and indeed the only one with whom she had any even chance of happiness. To her credit she came quickly to know, if not to admit this; and what she had undertaken as a concession—"Well, for God's sake, I've got to marry someone"—she recognized to be a choice supported by a cosmic inarticulate wisdom. And when he died, five years before this, struck down in midstride as they took together the evening air, departing as quietly as you please, his hand never leaving hers, she felt that she had died too and that she held on now in the flesh only because, as always, she was not as brave as he was. Her tartness, her constitutional intolerance, her unwillingness to compromise, had been intensified by that sad event and the solitude which followed it; and Bertie Waddell among others, a fool but no masochist, had long since removed Helen Blankenship from her social round. It distinguished the committee, therefore, and boded well for the success of its mission, that she had consented under pressure to sit upon it. She was what every committee needs; she was the snapping dog to keep the sheep together, those sheep whose something of themselves, of which they were scarcely cognizant, when shorn, would be the work they had been convoked to do. Whatever her contempt for her fellows, however, she had dressed in a manner to curry favor with them. Her dress of gray cashmere fitted well her light, almost girlish body. A rose-colored silk scarf hid the wrinkles in her throat. The application of eye shadow had softened her face and stopped, if it had not reversed, its tendency in her later years to resemble more and more closely a hawk's. She was as beautiful at sixty-six as she had ever been.

The others members of the committee were not so much late to arrive, tho now they were threatening to become that, as Mrs. Blankenship had been early. As usual, she had something to say, one of the usual things, which she had just got to because Mrs. Owings had not long before forbidden her to broach the subject again. "And," she was saying, "I suppose we shall be favored with Rita's presence?"

"Now Helen," admonished Mrs. Owings, anticipating the event and failing completely to hide her amusement, "do be fair."

"I am fair. That is the problem. I have been remarkably fair. And still I do not trust her."

Mrs. Owings very sensibly inquired, "What's there not to trust? What difference does either make in any case?"

Mrs. Blankenship produced her reasons and made them sound ominous. "I don't trust her motives. I know she hasn't a care in the world for the church. How could she?"

Mrs. Owings made light of her friend's objection: "Honestly, Helen! Her motives are none of my concern, nor should they be of yours. Her interest and her industry are. I sometimes feel that we wouldn't have gotten on without her. Besides"—she paused imperceptibly for the effect—"I've never noticed that you are the most devoted daughter of the church."

Mrs. Blankenship defended herself in peremptory fashion. "You will admit there is a difference, however. And I have been just as important to the project as she has." Then pausing, calling for her own effect, she defied contradiction. "Have I not?"

Mrs. Owings hastened to mollify her. "I am certain of it, Helen. The restoration would never have been done at all without you. You have been the conscience of the group. The beneficial conscience. You have not stopped things; you have made things go."

Mrs. Blankenship was not sure that she should allow herself to be bought off so easily. "That doesn't help, however true it might be. And you may stop trying to butter me up. You know I have a weakness for fattening things. And I'm not really sure I trust you any more than I trust her."

Mrs. Owings was enjoying herself. "Well, you may be right not to trust me, but that's exactly why I must butter you up. I wanted to ask a favor of you. Your help in a small matter."

"Oh no," interjected Mrs. Blankenship, already drawing a disapproving face, "I don't think I want to hear this."

But Mrs. Owings forged ahead, undeterred. "I've

decided to put Rita's name in for the Belles Dames."

"You wouldn't!" exclaimed an incredulous Mrs. Blankenship, genuinely caught off her guard. "You simply wouldn't."

"Oh but I would," was the assured response. "And what's more: I want you to help me get her in."

Mrs. Blankenship had all but lost her voice and could only sputter, "Never. I simply won't."

At this moment, the mellifluous chime in the foyer announced the arrival of another member of the committee. Mrs. Blankenship could think of nothing to add to her assertion but the comment, "Liz, this is too much. I'm surprised at you."

"But don't be, Helen. You've always said yourself that the club is a snake pit. I thought you might enjoy throwing her into it."

"Not when I'm one of the snakes," rejoined Mrs. Blankenship sharply.

This finally was too much for Mrs. Owings, and the amusement she had contained now bubbled over in a tinkling laugh not unharmonious with the rich stately tones of the chimes which seemed still to reverberate through the room. That was the attitude she was caught in—her head thrown delicately back, her small even teeth delicately exposed—when Willie May entered and announced grandly, in a manner befitting that she wore a starched gray uniform (tho ill befitting that her plump brown body and her impertinence almost popped the buttons of it), "Mrs. Lazarus."

"Ah Rita," said Mrs. Owings rising. "How good of you to come. We were just talking of you."

"Indeed," said Mrs. Lazarus. "I hope the conversation has been edifying. How are you, Helen?"

"We were just wondering at your devotion to the church," observed Mrs. Blankenship, accepting the advantage offered but failing to extend the usual courtesies in her haste to get on with it.

Mrs. Lazarus hesitated just a moment before saying: "I wonder at it myself sometimes."

"I'm glad that you arrived first," Mrs. Owings said, acting the conspiratress. "I've been trying to teach Helen a little tolerance and find that I need allies."

"None's likely to help," discouraged Mrs. Blankenship. "I'm too old to start tampering with my opinions now."

Mrs. Owings stated a principle: "One is never too old for a little diplomacy."

Mrs. Blankenship promptly made known her opinion on that score. "Diplomacy is the policy of the vulnerable—those with something to hide or those too weak to get their way by other means."

Mrs. Owings inquired, "Oh, then, do you always get your way?"

Mrs. Blankenship answered, "Heavens, no. Why do you think I'm a Christian?"

Mrs. Lazarus saw fit to interject, "I'm afraid, Liz, I'm not going to be much help to you. I've never understood why people do become Christians. I can do nothing for Helen's education."

Mrs. Blankenship made bold to have the last word, as usual, before Mrs. Owings signaled a halt to the discussion and offered tea to the new arrival. "Don't worry, Rita. There aren't that many of us. It's not worth your trouble to understand so few."

Mrs. Lazarus accepted the offer of libation with some faint hesitancy, an infinitesimal catch of the breath, as if to remind herself that one could not be too careful and those others, whoever they might be, that she was different. Those others scarcely needed the reminder, certainly not one so redundant of so many like it. But then understatement was one of the graces Mrs. Lazarus chose to exercise only occasionally. Certainly today she had chosen otherwise. She had dressed to stand apart. In flamboyant contrast to the black and white always affected by Mrs. Owings and the dove gray of Mrs. Blankenship, she had clothed her short stocky body in a dress of light blue suede which clashed loudly with the bright orange tint of her hair, a finely spun orange bubble much like a motorcyclist's helmet, and the lavender of her lipstick. Bertie Waddell was terribly envious of the expense invested in Mrs. Lazarus' wardrobe—"What I could do with that amount of money!" she had exclaimed petulantly to Mrs. Owings on more than one occasion—and only included her rival on her round because she had to have somewhere to go, even if it required rising above her principles, and because she knew she faced no challenge from that quarter. What she did face, what they all faced, tho those who recognized it were too proud or too sensible to admit it, was the relentless accusation Mrs. Lazarus leveled at her, at them, for her being set apart.

The foyer chime again emitted its golden glow, and in due course Willie May appeared to announce Mr.

Huxley and Father Tattersall. The former of these gentleman, an attorney by profession and by acclamation the possessor of the most distinguished bearing in town, was but recently embarked on his second term as mayor. His jurisdiction did not include the ground on which the proposed restoration stood, nor could the original movers and shakers of the project expect any material support from the good Scotch tax base on which he rose. He was rumored, moreover, to be incapable of suscitating ideas of his own, incapable further of recognizing his expropriation (for the public good) of others' ideas. But the ones he came by were already pretty common knowledge by the time he got his hands on them, and no one but the most ornery and contumacious begrudged him his happy, almost childlike possession of them. Mrs. Blankenship of course was one: What do we need with a maidenhead? she had asked. And Mrs. Owings had had to array her arguments carefully to win her friend's concession: It will open bigger political doors, if we seem to have the community behind us, she had said; the community represented by its first citizen, the mayor. It had helped that she had appreciated Mrs. Blankenship's little play on words, for if that redoubtable lady was above the practice of diplomacy herself she was by no means below its being practiced on her. It had helped finally that tradition was with Mrs. Owings: one could not engage in activity with political overtones without appearing to subvert the government, and Mrs. Blankenship was the staunchest of Republicans, tho among the first to admit that fools and blackguards were sometimes called, one hoped mistakenly, to fill the posts her party claimed. Mrs. Owings' arguments appeared now to be vindicated. The sixth member of the committee was an emissary from the governor, whom the mayor had called eight weeks before, as one classmate to another, to describe the project and solicit the state's assistance. The governor felt kindly toward the mayor, thought he owed him at least one, as it were, for his fecklessness, for the ease with which he lost difficult cases (to the benefit of the governor's clients when, younger, the two men had opposed each other in the courtroom) and the difficulty he had with easy ones, and promised his support. When she heard of that support, Mrs. Blankenship expressed her pleasure that at last they had found something Neville could do: not persuade a judge on the merits of a case, nor bully and win his way, nor call in old debts (he had no idea he had obliged anyone), but gamble like a fool with some-one else's money: I can just hear him now, can't you? Much obliged to you, Ted, and Ted, by all accounts, not a man to take another's admission of an obligation lightly, he's probably already calculated what use he can put us all to. Mrs. Owings had told her friend then not to be cruel, but her laughter as she spoke the reprimand blunted its barb. In fact she wanted the matter dropped for she didn't want her own motives looked into. She, she felt, was also one of those in Neville Huxley's unwitting debt. He had had the ves-tigial good sense, thirty-odd years before and while still a law student, to follow his mother's advice and be-come the most ardent suitor of the beautiful, tho quietly straitened, former Miss Elizabeth Bolton. The present Mrs. Owings was not without her vanities altogether; and that a young man of promise had once been in love with her, even if that love had been manifested in a most obstreperous manner and had required that on one occasion she cool his ardor with a spicy slap across the chops, endeared him to her always.

"Neville, how good to see you," said Mrs. Owings extending her hand and presenting her cheek to be kissed simultaneously.

"You are as beautiful as ever, Liz, as beautiful as ever," said Mr. Huxley, bowing his large head with its white mane and Roman nose and soft brown eyes and full expressive lips to do the honors.

"And Father, how good of you to come," she continued, having accepted that token of esteem, tho wondering now as she often wondered whether Neville even recalled that he had once prostrated himself before her, whether the token was in remembrance of that or merely the habit whose inception he could not recall and whose persistence he did not question. "We've been having some tea. Won't you join us?"

Had the founders of the committee striven to give it balance of form and personality, they could not have chosen better than to yoke together Neville Huxley and Casper Tattersall. The Father was short, lean, sallow, dark of hair, bright of dark eye, quick of movement and of mind, melancholy of temperament, ironical of mode, sharp of tongue when he chose to unsheath it. That was less seldom than he knew he should. But the blade was oiled with the familiar homilies of the church and went in and out without the complete knowledge of his victim, whose own discomfort that unfortunate could readily explain by the working of his conscience or the aptness of the Father's message to his case. He dressed of course, in his official capacity, in black, but allowed himself in winter the addition of a walking hat of Irish wool and in summer a Ben Hogan golf hat. To finish the image of the out-of-doors, he carried frequently a heavy walking stick. He had chosen to limit his vision of the world; but within that range he was honest, honest also with himself when the things he had excluded clamored to be heard, when the doubts began to muster. He suffered from a mild addiction to nicotine and was the only one of their acquaintance, since her husband had died, to be able to hold his own in combat with Mrs. Blankenship. At this moment he took matters more or less into his own hands. "A glass of sherry, perhaps."

"But of course," Mrs. Owings replied; asked, "Neville?"

Mr. Huxley, pretending not to impose: "Oh anything, anything at all will do."

"Rita? Helen? A touch more?"

There was a moment of silence during which each lady paused to hear what the other would say, the better to contradict it by her own example; then their policies reconsidered and having tried to anticipate what the other would say, again with the intention of contradicting it, each spoke up first: "Yes, please, but only half a cup."

As the other greetings and prefatory comments were being exchanged, Mrs. Owings busied herself with the refreshments at the tea wagon which Willie May had wheeled into the room shortly after Mrs. Blankenship arrived. She enjoyed this social ritual; and since she now had few opportunities to perform it, she slowed her preparations and savored each stage of the process: the splash of hot liquid on fine china, the clean smell of lemon, the glitter of sugar. There was something supremely refined about the taking of tea, she thought, something which bespoke one's easy intercourse with high culture—the ancient Chinese, the Georgian English. She did not feel the need for a more intimate acquaintance with other civilizations than that she had, that filtered first by the great American institutions, its museums and department stores, and then enriched by her own imagination. To have gained more would have required too much discomfort, the indignity of making one's needs known to mute, inhospitable strangers, the disruption of the uneasy understanding she had with the functions of her body. The most distant country she herself had visited was Canada. A travel poster had lured her and her husband to Banff for their honeymoon and they had returned there a number of times for vacations, just the two of them, leaving the children at home. She still exchanged Christmas cards with a few of the friends they had made there. Her own desires and proclivities aside, however, she did see the point in perpetuating the customs and adapting the symbols of those times and places of which she approved. There was a point to preserving beauty, even beauty of gesture. The principle was that round which the committee ostensibly rallied now. She could just see the bowed heads of the faithful and just know there was supreme value in honoring them in this manner. The symbols, the polished gestures—these were the things by which she marked the progress of the species. In a rare moment of inspiration once at a party, Neville Huxley had opined that what the world lacked was simple kindness, that he had observed how seldom people were kind to each other; and she had found herself nodding vigorously in agreement. Well, this was her solution to the problem. She doubted that kindness could be taught, but certainly the form of kindness could, the polished gestures could be imposed. And then one could hope for the best, hope that eventually conduct had an effect on character. In the meantime, one could punish the recusant.

Handing round the refreshments, she heard that the conversation had turned perforce to the subject of their final member. Mrs. Lazarus was saying, apparently in response to another's request for information, that her son Harold and he, a Mr. Max Bunting, had been at law school together. Mrs. Owings' stepping again into the circle they formed caused other facts to fall into place and she interrupted her report to exclaim, "But Liz, Loren must know him too, then. What did Loren say about him?"

Mrs. Owings hesitated a moment before answering, as if intent on her duties as hostess. "Loren said he has all the earmarks of a fine lawyer," she said and paused again, a pause Mr. Huxley hastened to fill: "Now there. I knew Ted wouldn't let us down. I knew he'd send us a good man."

She continued without taking note of Mr. Huxley's comment. "Loren also suggested that I hide the silver or at least count it after he left. He even offered to dig the hole for me in the backyard."

Mrs. Blankenship laughed, cried out with delight. "My sweet Loren! Where is thy lamp?"

Mrs. Lazarus cast her gaze down and to the side. Mr. Huxley reddened, sputtered, coughed; placed his mind upon the rack. Father Tattersall lit a cigarette and asked for another glass of sherry. The chime in the foyer sounded before Mrs. Owings had finished filling the Father's glass from the decanter on the tea wagon and before Mrs. Blankenship's hearty laughter had subsided. Mrs. Lazarus' wary gaze, oddly at odds with the smile she had drawn like a curtain across her face, had risen from its inspection of the splendid Bokhara on which rested her plump feet in blue pumps too small for them. Mr. Huxley, breathing hard like a locomotive hauling its train up a hill, continued to press his mind for a riposte or an explanation, either of which might get him off the hook he had clambered on to but neither of which might prove offensive to his hostess. His right hand assisted the process by running slowly back and forth along the line of his face indicated by his left jawbone. Father Tattersall patted his lips with the linen handkerchief he always carried in the breast pocket of his jacket for perhaps the dozenth time since entering the room. Willie May appeared and, this time smiling with embarrassment, for reasons only to be surmised, announced Mr. Bunting.

"Ah Mr. Bunting," said Mrs. Owings gliding toward him, "we were beginning to wonder whether you would find the place."

He was a vaguely handsome young man of medium height with no poor feature and no distinctive one. His hair was black and moderately cut and showed a tendency to curl, which independence he had attempted to tame with a vigorous brushing and the liberal use of hair oil; he was so closely shaved that his skin glistened; he wore tortoiseshell glasses of a low power of magnification. His suit, navy blue with pinstripes, was finely tailored; it was impossible to tell, so long as he kept his vest buttoned, that he had begun (and reasonably well advanced) to acquire the extra flesh around the middle that denotes the end of youth and the attainment of standing in the professional world; no flakes of dandruff on his shoulders gave him away; a silk tie in a paisley print added color and panache to the ensemble. He wore a wafer-thin gold watch, which it was his habit to consult, on his left wrist, and on the middle finger of his right hand, a silver ring set with a lapis lazuli. His story was that the ring was a family heirloom given him by his grandmother as she drew near her death and worn for deep sentiment. But the legend had passed among his fellow students (a legend supported by the common conviction that he had been hatched from an egg) that he had bought it in a pawnshop, in the manner of an Italian count his pedigree, and wore it on that finger to remind himself which one he was to raise in the famous puritanic gesture of anger and contempt (the worst plague one could wish on anyone) when he felt those emotions bursting in his breast and sorely in need of expression. He perspired now, a fine glaze over his perpetually earnest forehead; and perspiring he took Mrs. Owings' proffered hand and said, "Mrs. Owings, I presume. I'm terribly sorry to be late."

She sought to assure him. "Our directions, I'm afraid, were not the best."

"By no means," he sought the onus for himself. "I came just as you described. The problem was that I was rather late getting away, and perhaps drove a bit fast in hurrying to make up the time. I can assure you that our streets and highways are adequately patrolled. I spent a lot of time talking myself out of two different speeding tickets."

Mrs. Owings made use of this interesting relevation. "If you were successful, you should give Mrs. Blankenship your secret. She could use a little gilding on her tongue and long ago gave up keeping track of her traffic citations. Isn't that right, Helen?"

Mrs. Blankenship, pleased to have the first word, even at the expense of admitting her peccadilloes and revealing her propensities, drew an indignant expression across her sharp little face and broke into a rash of rhetorical questions: "Is it my fault they are out to get me? Is it my fault they lie in wait for me? Is it my fault I wrote a letter to the paper to excoriate them for their incompetence when they failed to recover the jewels stolen from my home? Is it my fault I see fit to speak my mind? Is it my fault if I was born with a heavier foot than the next lady? My rights and these differences are not taken into account. But I suppose I must be realistic. If you've a secret, do share it with us. I'm Helen Blankenship."

"Mrs. Blankenship, Max Bunting," he said stepping forward and taking her fine, small-boned hand in his moist one. "My secret's no great secret. It helps to have in your possession an identity card with your affiliation with the governor's office printed boldly on it. To that add the look of having great things to do in a great hurry."

"Ah," said Mrs. Blankenship, "I shall have to see about one of those cards. The government still owes me a big one anyway. The look I was born with; it's the genuine article."

Her reference to the indebtedness of the government—any government: federal, state or local—to her only Mrs. Owings would understand. She still bore the grudge, as had her husband throughout his life, that he, a superb research chemist, had been drafted into service in World War II for his formidable skills at the age of thirty-four and then, grave insult to injury, by some typical snafu, had been shipped overseas to fill the front ranks of the liberators. He had returned unscarred, but not unscathed, and a rabid Rupublican for life.

The introductions proceeded. It was obvious that Mr. Bunting had prepared himself well. He asked Mrs.

Lazarus immediately about the fortunes of his friend and classmate, her son Harold, tho custom and courtesy to the others required that he hear only that he was doing fine. He conveyed the governor's personal regards to Neville Huxley and his, that is, the state's, thanks that its citizens took these matters into their own hands, by which Mr. Huxley, smiling, felt strangely vindicated and let off the hook, to which he responded, his huge hands enveloping and pumping Mr. Bunting's well circulated one, grown moister from the exercise, with the repetition: "And mine to him. And mine to him." He showed the proper respect for Father Tattersall, who hoped that he had as much good advice for the rest of them as he had had for Mrs. Blankenship, to which Mr. Bunting replied that he was an intermediary only and therefore not charged to give advice, to which Father Tattersall responded that, then, their—his own and Mr. Bunting's—jobs were similar, that they therefore could understand each other, that finally, tho his advice were not official, they could hope for an amount of interpretation from Mr. Bunting as his parishioners could hope for that from him, at which Mr. Bunting, suspecting that his leg was being pulled, murmured and fell silent. He took lemon in his tea when his preference was sought; he politely took the room's least-comfortable chair despite Mrs. Owings' urging and set his briefcase, a splendid object in chestnut-colored leather with brass fittings and his initials embossed below the handle, at his feet.

When the settling down was completed and Mr.

Bunting held his cup upon his knee and Father Tattersall's glass had been replenished, Mrs. Owings opened the business: "It was terribly kind of you to come, Mr. Bunting."

"Well, the governor takes a great personal interest in our state's heritage. Perhaps you know he makes a hobby of collecting arrowheads and Confederate money and that sort of thing. But even if he himself did not, he feels it's important that the state support this kind of endeavor. The past must be preserved—"

"That sounds just like Ted," Mr. Huxley interjected, smiling his approval, one suspected, of himself, but then did not elaborate what sounded like him nor explain why it was important to verify what no one else in the room had thought to doubt and left an awkward little pause in the conversation which Mrs. Owings filled presently, her eyes beginning glow more intensely. "We're quite excited about the project ourselves. The church is such a dear little thing, so droopy and forlorn and in need of repair. And then we all believe passionately that there is a first good to be done in keeping these old things up. Helen has expressed it very well."

Mrs. Blankenship made claim to her rights. "I'm perfectly capable of carrying my own ball when I see fit to. I'm sure Mr. Bunting does not care to know all our thoughts on the subject."

Mr. Bunting saw the opportunity to ingratiate himself to both parties and took it. "On the contrary, anything at all which would allow me to see the matter more clearly would be helpful."

Thus reproved, however gently, seeming suddenly like a child made to recite a poem she knew by heart, Mrs. Blankenship perhaps blushed and surely said, shaking her head, "Oh, it's really nothing all that startling. Just that one finds in the church such a human dimension."

"Well put indeed, Helen," approved again Mr. Huxley, puffing up his lips in contemplation of that place described, like heaven, which he had never seen but always meant to visit.

"God is always mindful of his children," Father Tattersall put in.

For Mrs. Owings that was not enough and she pursued the matter eagerly. "Oh, but the way you said it, Helen. When we first came upon the church and pushed open that old door on its rusty hinges. It was quite moving, quite beautiful."

Mr. Bunting subtly impugned his previous statement and implied that some of those things included within the category of anything at all were less important than others when he asked, "How did you find the church, by the way?"

Mrs. Owings answered promptly and called for reinforcements. "Rita, perhaps you could tell Mr. Bunting."

Mrs. Lazarus began tentatively. "I think really that Helen should be the one."

Mrs. Blankenship bristled to think that anyone might take her side in the matter. "Not at all, Rita, if this is what Liz wants. You needn't worry about me. I shall have my say when the time comes."

"I never doubted that, Helen. But I thought that, since you were the first one on the scene—"

Again Mrs. Blankenship interrupted her, in contest for the martyr's laurels: "But you were the one to turn up the old records after all, and so you are the one best able to paint the background for Mr. Bunting."

"As you wish," began Mrs. Lazarus, making a small mistake in the interest of establishing her innocence, which mistake Mrs. Blankenship, drawing a lugubrious face, could not let pass without notice taken of it. "My wishes have long since ceased to be of any consequence to anyone except myself." There was nothing for Mrs. Lazarus to do but acknowledge the plea with a perfunctory, "Ah well," and then to continue: "The church came first to our attention about two years ago—"

Mrs. Blankenship murmured, "Twenty-six months."

Mrs. Lazarus accepted the correction gracefully. "Twenty-six months ago, when Amos Miller died and his nephew, who now lives in Cincinnati, came home to settle the estate. Of course this isn't home for him and never has been. His mother married and moved away and bore him away from here; and before he came back this time, no one here could remember his ever having set foot in town. As it turned out, as a boy he had visited his uncle and the family ground once, and he remembered a surprisingly good deal about the town. But that was long ago, and his roots are elsewhere now, and he has no interest in moving back here. All—"

Mrs. Blankenship's patience reached its limit, and

she fairly burbled, her eyes wide with indignation. "I think Mr. Bunting should know something about the Millers and their land."

Mrs. Lazarus replied serenely, "I was just coming to that. The Millers—"

Mrs. Blankenship: "Finally. I admit I had my doubts."

Mrs. Lazarus, losing patience herself: "No one doubts that, Helen. Your doubts are famous but about as good for anything as white bread."

Then, before Mrs. Blankenship could make something of that, she proceeded to tell Mr. Bunting the story of how the Millers' land came into being, came into being so far as they were concerned, they and their forebears, ignorant of natural history and prior claim and the simple justice of leaving things as they are, the land and the church which stood upon the land. Mrs. Blankenship chose not to interrupt further, tho whether chastened or bored or content that Mrs. Lazarus at last had her facts in order one could not say. The expression attending those three attitudes and many others besides was the same. The story, according to Mrs. Lazarus at least, took some thirty minutes to tell.

The first public record of the Millers dated from the early 1840's. That document was a deed for the property on which the church now stood. All records and all surmise indicated that they were an independent and a religious clan; and as they accumulated more property, they memorialized and sanctified that first plot, tore down the building on it and constructed a church to God's glory and their honor. They completed the structure in 1849 and called it Oak Grove Church. Its congregation seemed to have been comprised of family and immediate neighbors willing to worship as the Millers dictated and at any one time as many as forty slaves. They seemed to have embraced no denomination; their creed was their own and they worshiped God in their own way with the assistance of a piano hauled up from Charleston and installed in 1854. There was no record that an ordained minister was ever called to the church, nor that any other outside influence was felt until the outbreak of the War between the States.

Independent-minded among a rebellious people, self-sustaining at a social level well below that of those who had become dependent for their wealth and preeminence on Northern or European manufacture, the Millers suffered few of their men to go off to fight another's battle. Their upcountry domain kept them pretty much out of the way of the various armies drifting like a pestilence over the entire region. Their own numbers stood them in good stead against the marauders and bands of deserters from both sides whose misfortune it was to happen by. When the war ended, they found themselves pretty much intact and, in contrast to the legends, ready to profit. They knew the ultimate value of the land, and in those years immediately after the war they exerted themselves to add to their extensive holdings. What they could, they simply laid claim to; that demonstrably in another's hands, they wheedled, extorted, traded for, or, if all else failed, bought. Their Negroes they kept on to help them work the land at poorer wages, or the equivalent thereof, and under poorer conditions than those which prevailed before the emancipation. It was now estimated that at one time shortly after the turn of the century, the Miller clan, as they had come singularly to be known, for convenience, after marrying Knoxes and Cathcarts and Johnsons and Bishops, owned and controlled one-fifth of the land in Lexington county. Their mistake and the seed of their downfall, however, were to remain independent-minded. Some married poorly and against the advice of their families; others invested poorly and without the benefit of advice. The holdings were parceled out as more sons wanted land of their own; the old bonds of blood began to fray. No one thought to enter politics, except an occasional renegade son who saw the easy life to be lived and the ready profit to be made as a law enforcement officer, and thus to bind the splintering empire together by his wider authority; no one sought an education beyond the rudiments of bookkeeping; no one learned the first rules of leadership—how to command loyalty from a collection of dissidents incapable of perceiving individually the coincidence of their interests. The infrequent family reunions were fiascoes marked by fistfights and the destruction of property and, following the last recorded gathering, a horrible automobile crash, which depleted their number by four young strong but worthless males. By the time of the Depression, only the ground claimed almost a century before, the church ground and its six hundred surrounding acres, could survive the beating.

Amos Miller, the owner of that land, was a recluse and believed to be insane. In fact what he was was fiercely proud of his ancestors—their courage, their tenacity, their independence, their vision—and equally fiercely contemptuous of their descendants, the feckless, complaining, ignorant sycophants who had squandered their gifts. He had refused all intercourse with his cousins, near and far, to the point, when it became necessary, of running off, with a shotgun, a good number of them who had gone out to his place as supplicants—fathers, mothers, and children alike. He himself never married, a fact which excited no surprise, since it was generally agreed that no woman in her right mind would have him. What did surprise those who knew it was the affectionate address to his nephew in his will, a young man he had not seen in twenty-one years but with whom he had corresponded throughout that time and especially since the death of the lad's mother. The assessment of his various competences was already too well established, however, to alter the judgment against him. It could be reasonably asked that, if the young man had loved the old man so, why had he not visited him more often. The love therefore could be seen as quirk, aberration, another clinical symptom. Few people ever saw Amos Miller, and no one did who did not go out to Miller's Corners about nine miles west of the city of Lexington.

For forty years he lived off the revenues from leasing his land to the International Paper Company and the labor and care of a Negro couple who belonged as much to the land as he did himself. They did most of the shopping, even buying, infrequently to be sure, the piece of farm machinery from the John Deere man, and all the banking and the worshiping; the negotiating with the paper company Mr. Miller did himself, at each renewal making the company's agent walk all over the property with him to verify that they had not already cut more trees than they were allowed. How he spent his days no one knew or cared until he died. He and all but those two or three of the rest of the world shared a disregard for each other which his retreat and its willingness to let him go uncontested could only gratify. There was evidence at the end, however, to suggest that the world had been the loser in the exchange: the pleasant young man, his nephew, who, tho he had not visited his uncle in years, appeared stricken by the news of his death and embarrassed by the legacy; the copious tears shed by Horace and Sadie Buncombe, tho he had left them well provided for; the huge library he had acquired through the Book-of-the-Month Club, which he had requested to be burned rather than allow it to fall into the hands of a populace he despised. Given that, the greater surprise contained in his will, duly signed and certified, tho by no means beyond challenge by an even modestly able attorney, was the stipulation that the old church be restored and made to stand as a memorial to those of his clan who first came to this country and by extension, if one wanted to assume so, to all its early settlers. The continuing lease of the land was to provide funds for the restoration and maintenance of the structure; the Buncombes, if they chose to accept the position, would serve as its custodians; to Lawrence Goodwin would go any difference between the revenues gained and the costs incurred, as well as the substantial sum old Amos had saved, minus the one hundred dollars bequeathed, with the contemptuous gesture of a lord scattering pennies before peasants to distract them, to his other relations.

Mrs. Lazarus drew to the conclusion of her story. "It's his distant kin, all those Cathcarts and Bishops and all, who have kept us from getting on with the project. But now that obstacle seems to be removed. The courts have denied their last claim. We, the committee here, called together by the Lexington County Historical Association when Lawrence Goodwin called us with the news, have solicited estimates on the restoration from several reputable firms—one from Savannah, one from Charleston, one from Atlanta. We've studied what few examples of ecclesiastical architecture of that era exist in these parts, tho they've not contributed much to our understanding, since Oak Grove is one of a kind. The plans, if there ever were any, have long since disappeared. But the remarkable thing is that the building is pretty much intact, at least so far as we can tell. The restoration people told us that the two worst things for buildings, other than their owners, are weather and vandals; and old Amos seems to have had his own way with at least one of those. So, we think we're all set. We only need your, uh, the state's, uh, approval."

"Approval?" queried Mr. Bunting.

"Approval's not really the right word," took up Mrs. Owings eagerly. "What we want is an official designation."

"Ah," said Mr. Bunting.

Mrs. Owings explained, the passion and the triumph resonant in her voice: "We want the governor to declare the church a state historical landmark."

"I see," said Mr. Bunting; and then, since he did not elaborate, an uncomfortable silence ensued, during which the ladies of the committee crept forward in their chairs, Mr. Huxley cleared his throat and subsided further into his, and Father Tattersall lit another cigarette, noticed the many butts already crowding the ashtray at his elbow, and bestirred himself to empty its contents into the smoldering fire. The emissary pinched and pulled his lower lip in a gesture of contemplation, regarded each member of the committee in turn, and tantalized all but the splendid indifferent, the mayor, with the nature of his unrevealed thoughts. At last he spoke. "You know, of course, that that kind of designation is very difficult to come by. It is something not given to every rude shack in the woods. It is an important statement by this administration."

There was vigorous nodding all around.

"Ahem," he continued when no one spoke to break the tension and relieve him of the responsibility. "Now let me get this straight. The money has been put up already."

Again there was nodding.

Again there was silence.

Mr. Bunting mused, with more desperation than he showed, "That might make a difference."

Glances, barely hopeful, were exchanged.

Mr. Bunting marked time. "Ah, what is the condition of the church presently?"

Mrs. Blankenship, murmuring, unable to control herself: "At present."

Mrs. Owings to the attack: "It is in very poor repair. It must be entirely redone, almost board by board. But all three restoration companies agree that the original foundation—imported brick, would you believe, used as ballast in the ships from England early in the last century?—will support the work. Why, even the original piano is in place, the pulpit, most of the pews, some of the glass."

Mr. Bunting: "And how long will the work of restoration take?"

To this Mrs. Owings responded shortly, as if growing impatient with questions of little importance, the extended preliminaries, "The average is two years."

"Ah," said Mr. Bunting; then stopped, then started. "But now I must ask the difficult question. Has the church any historical significance? I mean, did anything actually happen there?"

This was what they had all been waiting for; but at the critical moment, with so much to bring to bear, Mrs. Owings found that her voice had deserted her.

Her mind worked feverishly, but no words gushed from her lips. And Mr. Bunting, suddenly afraid that he had offended, made matters worse by stating his advocacy for the devil in cruder and far less sympathetic terms, in a voice which had risen noticeably in register. "I mean, what really is the point?"

"God's children prayed there when the land was a wilderness," declared Father Tattersall with the maddening calm of the apologist.

"Ah yes but," began Mr. Bunting, aware of his rudeness and blushing slightly in spite of himself, but unwilling to make amends for his trespass or otherwise admit that he was in error and so forced to continue as he had inadvertently begun.

"No," Mrs. Owings, interrupting, urged, her strange little lapse brought abruptly to an end, "Father Tattersall has a point, a good point. We have here the evidence—moldering tho it may be—the evidence of how ordinary lives were lived. A people much like ourselves worshiped in this place. We ourselves could have done it had we been of the time and place. For ourselves then, we ought to preserve the evidence. We ought not to lose touch with that people like ourselves. We ought to do this to assert our own importance. The great are preserved in museums and textbooks and what all. They have little need of our care. But our abandoned church is the promise of our own lives— that we will somehow be acknowledged by and important for our descendants. I think we all hope that one hundred and fifty years from now, the people then living will be kind enough and sensitive enough to want to know how we lived and how close we are to them."

The other members of the committee knew very well indeed Mrs. Owings' commitment to the project; but they, with the exception of Mr. Bunting, who felt something as a bug must feel to be impaled on the end of a pin by a wanton boy, knew also her usual manner—the ironical turn, the eyebrow raised in amusement—and the fervor with which she spoke astonished them. None supported her therefore. And it was left to Mr. Bunting to fill the vacuum which her rush of speech created. He adjusted his glasses in preparation, cleared his throat, looked askance as if in search of a place to hide, finally began uncertainly: "Ah yes, well yes. That is nice. That is nice indeed. Ah. I'm not sure I've been sufficiently empowered to promise you the state's help. But the governor is behind you, I can assure you that. And we will do what we can to make things easier for you."

He limped to a conclusion, resettled his glasses on his nose, shot a glance at each of the committee members in turn, wondered whether he had gone too far, all the time certain that he had been bullied mercilessly into going further than he had wanted or intended. He decided then that he detested and despised this woman and her coterie of friends, who had made it their business to catch him alone, to gang up on him, and to embarrass him. Well, nothing had gone down on paper or tape, he thought; and anything the governor was reluctant to give, he would simply deny having promised . . . Well, perhaps you misunderstood; I thought I was making myself clear . . . The sight of those pleased faces and the sound of those excited voices made him anxious, as always did the show of too much satisfaction among his antagonists. And he began finally to hate the governor, too, for sending him on this mission which the other lawyers in the office had laughed about and called his afternoon off. His final words were scarcely out of his mouth before Mr. Huxley exclaimed, "There. I told you. He is with us."

"Mr. Bunting, this is too kind," exclaimed Mrs. Owings, bringing her hands together in one gentle clap before her breast.

"How nice," said Mrs. Lazarus warily, "how terribly nice!"

Mrs. Blankenship saw fit to warn, "Well, let's hope the governor doesn't botch this as badly as he did that nuclear power thing."

"Let us pray," said Father Tattersall, patting his lips in preparation for his intercession with the Almighty.

Obediently the committee members bowed their heads and suffered a blessing on their project to be besought. A susurration of amens sealed the prayer presently. And they raised their heads, set again to murmur round their self-congratulations, to find Willie May on her knees among them. She contributed to and prolonged the general concurrence. "Amen, brother, a-a-men." Even as she knelt, she held an orange pound cake with a lemon glaze; and holding it, she had very much the look of offering it in sacrifice to the committee, who, one and all, watched her, speechless, with something of the morbid fascination one might feel to watch another defecate by the side of the road, until she had satisfied herself.

"A true daughter of the church," said Father Tattersall, moving quickly to help her rise.

Willie May said, with a note of challenge in her voice, "No one ever been known to pray too much."

"Willie May has made one of her cakes for us," announced Mrs. Owings, taking up the silver cake knife. "I'm sure I can prevail on you all to have a piece."

Willie May made quick to scotch objections before they could be expressed. "There won't nobody mind the extra weight."

As was to be expected, no one did mind, or at least said so, and Mr. Bunting offered his services to distribute the pieces Mrs. Owings cut. He had then ample opportunity to admire the heft of her silver and the delicacy of her china and to set in store enough of her good fortune, indeed her great fortune, for the full exercise of his envy on the way home; further, as audience to their antiphony, to participate in the philosophical discourse between Father Tattersall and Mrs. Blankenship on the tendency of television guests on television talk shows happily to confess their most intimate secrets, their alcoholism, their abortions, their sexual preferences and practices (*He*: There is a lot of it going around. Frankly I think we would do much better not to have all this public breast beating. *She*: You make it sound like a virus. *He, roguishly*: Well, an infection surely. A social disease.); further, to deny himself, with regret, the full description of how Mrs. Lazarus' son really was. At last he was free to express the hope to Mrs. Owings that he would have the chance to see Loren before he had to leave.

Mrs. Owings faced him squarely, smiled sweetly, and lied without hesitation. "Yes, he wanted to see you too. He had some business to attend to this afternoon, but hoped to return before you had to go."

Mr. Bunting, who suspected deception and betrayal everywhere, pursued, "He's doing well, I trust. This new firm seems to be catching on."

Mrs. Owings laughed. "Oh I suppose."

Mr. Bunting was quick to take the hint he presumed. "Oh? Is anything wrong?"

Again she laughed. "Oh no. Nothing like that. It's just that Loren has always been so self-contained that I've never felt I did know how things stood with him. But then they say a mother is always the last to know, don't they."

Mr. Bunting played the diplomat. "I suppose it depends on who they are and what it is that is known."

She honored him with a third laugh. "You are a delight, Mr. Bunting. I'm so glad the governor chose to send you."

Mr. Bunting adjusted his glasses on his nose and said, "Please call me Max."

Mrs. Blankenship and then the others were soon invited to share this intimacy as the normal shifting and sifting of the committee brought the young man again near each in turn; and in due course her old friend had

Mrs. Owings by the ear. "I do believe I have just been done a favor."

Mrs. Owings inquired, "Indeed?"

Mrs. Blankenship explained herself and ended haughtily, "I did not see fit to return it. What's good enough for the mailman is good enough for him."

Mrs. Owings said with little interest unfortunately, distracted by the sight of Rita Lazarus asking Willie May for her coat, "I should think so." Then moving forward, asked, "Rita, could you stay a minute? Helen and I have something to talk to you about."

Mrs. Blankenship, incredulous, made an attempt to restrain Mrs. Owings. "We do? I don't recall that we do."

Turning, as they gained the foyer together and established themselves just out of hearing of the men, Mrs. Owings smiled and said, "But of course, Helen, that plan of ours to put Rita up for the Belles Dames."

Mrs. Blankenship exclaimed, "Liz!"

Mrs. Owings insisted, "Certainly. You remember."

Mrs. Lazarus darted a glance in both directions and said, "Perhaps another time, Liz. I really must run now."

Father Tattersall and Mr. Huxley soon followed her lead and took their leaves with much good cheer and best wishes expressed all around. Mr. Bunting stayed on alone, and Mrs. Blankenship assumed the responsibility of keeping her friend company throughout the ordeal (confiding to her friend in process that she would keep her eye on the silver). Both thought that he held on in the hopes of having a word with Loren; and one at least wondered at the egotism (if he did not know) and the masochism (if he did) which kept him there to greet an acquaintance who reviled him. Both were wrong, however. And it came to pass presently that Mrs. Owings' child he saw was her daughter Susan. Toward five-thirty she bounded through the foyer, calling out in passing, "Hi Mom"; then, having been summoned into audience and caught herself up short, she swept into the salon and, to her mother's great surprise, embraced their guest and exclaimed, "Max, how lovely!" Some three hours later, after drinks and a hasty meal at the country club, the two young people contrived a sort of love on the front seat of his Mercedes-Benz. And there she repeated many times for his benefit, "Max, how lovely!" before, having consulted his watch over her shoulder, he affirmed that he really must be getting back to Columbia.

# 3

The peculiar light of one's consideration, impassioned or impartial, can make a mockery of the event; and already the shadow cast by his attention to the outrage of the night before had swelled and twisted and in process, inevitably, made the thing itself seem larger and more horrible than it was. It did not help that she had kept him from an immediate settling of accounts: No, she had implored, you'll wake them; he's gone anyway, I know he's gone. And he had had instead to comfort her as he could and to imagine the reasons for and the consequences of an occurrence either might have predicted but only at the risk of appearing to the other, after all their success, needlessly anxious or, worse, ready to break off the affair. He waited now for the telephone call he knew would come, waited impatiently, embittered, waited and plotted, and plotting became angrier and more bitter still. He knew he would not have to wait long; he knew his nemesis, no more than he, could endure the torture of a prolonged silence. He knew even how the call would be made: somehow Stanley would have gained access to the unlisted number of the private line—the number only a dozen people knew, mostly women; the number his colleagues called his hot line—and would use that. Even so, the loud harsh jangling of the instrument shortly after nine o'clock made him jump then grab the receiver before the instrument could ring a second time and shatter what nerves remained with the ludicrous ease of a hammer shattering icicles. He muttered a greeting. Stanley Sims' voice, chipper, fatuous, false, sounded so close to him that it seemed to emanate from his own head. "Loren? That you? You don't sound too good this morning. Didn't sleep too good, eh?"

Then he laughed with sincere amusement, and Loren made what feeble attack he could from his narrow corner. "You go to hell."

Stanley's voice shifted into tones of mocking blandishment. "Now wait a minute, wait a minute, Loren. Don't go 'n' get nasty on me. I'm calling to do you a favor. I have something of yours. You might call it the real you. And I just naturally thought you would want it back. But there are others who might want it too. And I just might see fit to let them have a peek if you get nasty."

Loren could do no better than to elaborate his previous statement. "You go to hell, you despicable pig. When I get my hands on you—"

But Stanley had little concern for that possibility. "Now just hold on there. Pigs is smart animals, and I won't have them talked about disrespectful. And I know you don't want to get me mad. It's all up to you. I's just trying to do you a favor."

Loren murmured, "You pig."

Stanley could almost be seen to shrug, "Well, if that's the way you want it."

The protasis dangled for two moments, three moments, as Loren tried to consider all the things he had run repeatedly through his mind during the previous seven hours; then he spoke sharply, desperately, "Wait."

That did not satisfy Stanley however; he asked, "Wait what?"

"You pig," he repeated; but the sorrow was too rich in his voice, and Stanley coaxed him rudely, "Now Loren."

He asked finally, "What do you want?"

Stanley reassumed his good cheer. "Now that's more like it. You see, I'm a fair-minded man. I don't want what don't belong to me. But it just naturally seem that I should have something for finding what don't belong to me. Now don't you think? Now don't that sound fair?"

The absurdity of these propositions made Loren become abstracted. He lost his sense of the moment and did not answer and presently the receiver erupted with angry words. "You listening to me, you cunt-sucker? I asked you don't that sound fair."

Still he did not answer. He felt a more pressing need for his badly diminished faculties than to engage in negotiations with a lunatic; he had to determine what would happen if the photographs fell into other hands than his own. His hand sought the reassuring smooth heaviness of the paperweight on his desk, the antique piece of glass which had sat, so he was told, on his grandfather's desk and which he kept more as a talisman, charmed and filled with secrets, his grandfather's wisdom, which he hoped someday to gain, than for its denominated use. He winced to imagine what the photographs revealed. He knew her body, his pleasure dome, the chapel of his prostration, better than he knew his own and was made sick to think of that dear face, that delicate body caught in that unforgiving light. He winced to think what they could not show: the truth about them, which no camera, despite the claims made for it, could capture. But the evidence, the lie itself, was not what distressed him. He knew their love and knew that it was strong enough to withstand this mockery of it. What he feared was the damage the apparent truth would do his mother if she encountered it in fact or rumor. He suspected she was not so strong as she seemed to those around her. There had been that year of silence, almost a year, after his father's death, and almost silence, instructions to the maid and almost nothing else. Yes, even rumor; and rumors there would be. The town would talk; it always did. Its citizens, with nothing else to distract them, would feast on the carrion they had made, by that, one could presume, to inoculate themselves against the same catastrophe's befalling them. There was no hope. They loved, as well, to see their betters, their equals even, brought low, for that promoted them. No. There was no hope. They would talk. There was no forgiveness in them, nor the dignity which would close their lips over the knowledge of another's disgrace. Disgrace: what disgrace in a love so pure? Still, how would it appear: the small room, the cheap furnishings, the two bodies aboard a single bed, asprawl it like the bare survivors of a shipwreck? To be caught so, did it not, did it not imply a willingness to be caught? Had they never locked the door? The trusting fools—

Stanley almost screamed, "You motherfucker, you listening to me?"

Loren said quietly, conceding, "Yes, I'm listening."

"Well, don't that sound fair?"

Loren strained to control his voice and paid it out in a thin brittle thread. "Yeah, Stanley. That sounds fair." Paused, amended, "It sounds as fair as a corpse smells like roses. It sounds as fair as you're capable of being. Now tell me how much you want."

Stanley giggled, "You always did have a way with words. I'm glad to see you're so smart too. That's going to make this real easy. As I said, I'm a fair-minded man. And I don't want more as what's coming to me natural. Now I don't know what value you place on your good name. It's kind of a hard thing to say. But I've put it at ten thousand dollars. How does that sound to you?"

Loren in fact felt relieved, thought for the first time that there might be an easy path out of the dilemma after all; he had called his man as he was, possessed of greed and addicted to the sound, the touch, the smell of money, and he had only once to gratify that lust, to make the payment and retrieve the photographs, to be rid of the problem, if not the man, forever. There lay the second problem: what was he to do with Stanley and, by extension, his family? But that could wait. Those photographs which he had not seen, for which he took Stanley's word, could not. His need for them was basic and as compelling as his need for food, the species' basic needs having grown in number as it shuffled off its instincts and strove to become civilized; his possession of them would afford a physical relief. Nor did the money pose a significant problem. It was a tidy sum, but one he could lay his hands on quickly and by a little creative accounting make disappear from his records. But still he could not move himself immediately to agree to these terms, to surrender, to place himself at Stanley's mercy. He said deliberately, "That sounds like a lot of money to me."

Again Stanley's voice swung wildly to vituperation. "You filthy bastard, you fucking jew. You got the money. I know you got the money. I seen you in the papers enough times, giving money to jews and niggers. What you ain't got is no dignity. You fuck my sister for free, and then you don't even have the decency to buy back your good name. You filthy bastards make me want to puke. Think you can do anything and get away with it because you got the money. But no fucking dignity. Well, you're going to learn it now. And you're going to learn it the hard way. The price has just gone up. It's twenty thousand now, twenty big ones. And no arguments or we end the whole thing right now and I drop the pictures in the mail." He laughed. "They're real good pictures. You'll like them. Just like *Playboy*." He laughed again. "Boy, for a man your size I didn't believe it. You got a cock on you the size of a baseball bat. I mean I never saw a nigger with a cock that size. No wonder my sister was doing it all for free."

Loren could control himself no longer. The dark bitter bile burst its organ. He clutched the paperweight, driving the veins of his wrist to the moist surface. He swore and promised, "Goddam you, I'll kill you for this."

But the anger seemed to gratify rather than to distress his enemy. The voice on the line cackled, "Now Loren. Don't go get all excited. I was just having a little fun. You know, you really shouldn't take things like that so seriously, a man in your position. I mean you got to learn to roll with the punches. Ain't no one ever told you that? Then you're getting more for your money than I thought. But what the hell. I'll just throw this in. A free lesson in how to get on in negotiations. You got to roll with the punches."

Stanley paused; but when Loren would not answer, he continued, as if unable to comprehend that reticence and that failure to perceive one's own interests. "I just don't understand it, Loren. I swear I don't. Here I'm just trying to do you a favor. Well, that's your business, I guess. You can do what you want. But one thing you're going to do is you're going to meet me at McClelland Park this afternoon. I want this to be all fair and square. I want you to see what you're getting for your money. You bring, well, let me see, how about five thousand. Yes, you bring me five thousand dollars at the pool in McClelland Park at four o'clock this afternoon and I'll show you what I got. If you like what you see, I'll tell you where you can get the rest of it. How does that sound?"

Loren said only, "I'll think about it."

Stanley expressed his surprise, his indignation, his continuing incomprehension. "What do you mean you'll think about it? I mean, what kind of man are you? Don't you have any dignity? I mean, don't you have any respect for yourself or for my sister? I simply don't believe it. Well, all I got to say is you better think fast and you better be there and you better have the money with you. Do you hear me?"

Loren heard him. But the elements of the fantastic and the macabre in their exchange were so vivid that for the moment his awareness of his circumstances deserted him; he seemed to float with the same confused attention of a somnambulist. He wondered at the febrile tingling in his extremities, the cold void where his viscera had been. And again Stanley waxed furious. "You listening, you motherfucker?"

At that Loren did recover speech; he spoke in a voice as soft and elusive as a vapor. "Yes, I'm listening. And I'll be there. There's only one thing, Stanley. If I were you, I'd bring my army."

He set the paperweight down as if affixing a period to his recommendation. Stanley laughed with malicious pleasure and continued to laugh and to repeat until Loren disengaged without another word. "Now that's a good one, Loren. That's a real good one."

Loren sat for many minutes after returning the receiver to its cradle with the consummate apparent calm of a chronic drunk restoring a chisel to its place. His hands quivered, another symptom of the illness which had stricken him. His head felt as if someone had placed a steel cap on it and then begun to tighten the screws until the bone beneath it began to crack. He clasped his hands and, resting his elbows on the desk, leaned his head gently, gingerly against them, catching his brows for support on his extended thumbs. He noticed other small rebellions against his authority: the dryness in his mouth, the ooze in his armpits, the terrific thumping of his heart. Neither would his mind be still, nor could he control it; it oscillated wildly from rage to fear and made faster swings the longer an answer took to present itself. What was he to do, what? He had not slept; he had cut himself shaving, while trying that morning to reimpose the usual order on his day. It was a very small nick and would not be noticed, except that, in his hurry, he had not waited for the wound to dry and a drop of blood had stained the collar of his otherwise immaculate white shirt. His fear of death had endured, unabating, for fifteen years: so sudden, so final, so unremitting, so little human. And yet now he courted it righteously. He had meant what he said. He swallowed hard once, twice, then noticed the cup of coffee, cold and still as polished marble, which his secretary had brought in with the first mail of the morning as was her habit on the stroke of nine. He sipped the coffee and, to his surprise, the tension began to ease. The worst of possibilities seemed that he would simply ransom the photographs for the demanded sum and burn them on the spot, and he wondered idly at the palliative properties of the drink at hand. He inferred that Stanley had no interest in anything but the money; it followed closely that he would do nothing to infringe his chances of getting it. What would follow that, within this worst of possibilities, he could not say. His present aim and purpose was simply to regain the evidence. He could do that. He breathed with greater ease.

His anger, however, his righteous anger, was not so readily appeased. Like a fabulous fire, the more it consumed, the more it found to sustain itself on; and that which, in other times and under other circumstances, would have excited his pity, his urge to understanding and relief, now became its fuel. Without the fear of discovery to restrain him, he began to invent and to consider alternative bests of possibilities. They had in common that they were to be retribution. He could not expect conscience to work this effect for him; so far as he could tell, Stanley was a man completely unencumbered by conscience. That assessment made his task easier. He had the responsibility to any living thing that the pain of punishment should be commensurate with the offense, that it should be for the offense and not for the pleasure derived from the witness of another's suffering. Even so, there was a difference between the punishments which could be meted out to men and animals, a difference perhaps only in the manner of their being meted out, but a difference. And that Stanley had no conscience certainly meant that he was something less than a man. The moral question stood in abeyance; the practical question was merely the choice to be made. After he had gained possession of the photographs, he must be certain that the money would be recovered or rendered useless or that Stanley would suffer for the possession of it. His mind, like a hungry hound baying with certain triumph, leapt upon the tracks of a half-dozen plans; but each showed quickly its false promise. To take the punishment into his own hands, to fight it out on the spot, was not so much to give Stanley his chance, a chance he did not deserve, according to the four or five inches and thirty or forty pounds that separated them, but to conduct matters by the villain's rules and not by his, the victim's: he preferred the subtle visitation, the punishment deferred; he wanted Stanley to walk away, thinking he had won, only to have the boom descend when he least expected it.

Of the first plans he turned up, however, none was without risks he was not willing to run. To pay the ransom in marked bills required Buddy Henderson's cooperation and Warren DeLorme's; and if Buddy owed him just about whatever he wanted (Buddy, who had been so indiscreet as to borrow money from his own bank at very favorable interest against collateral he did not possess and then not quite repay it all on time), the sheriff was incorruptible and, further, always in need of a reason for his doing anything. To pay the ransom in bills he had coated with poison, tho beautifully conceived to exploit Stanley's habit of sucking on his fingers, those fingers constantly begrimed with the various lubricants of an automobile, was to place at risk the ordinary citizens to whom Stanley gave the money before enough of the poison had accumulated in his system to end his career. To destroy the money by incendiary device, remotely controlled, required a more sophisticated knowledge of electronics and explosives than he possessed. To pay the ransom in counterfeit bills seemed at first to pose the same insuperable difficulties: acquisition of the device on such short notice, the involvement of others than himself and Stanley in the plot, Stanley's discovering the ruse before the last pictures had been recovered. But the longer he thought about it and as fewer became the plots he could spin on such short notice with any hope of success, the more favorably he looked at this and the more likely its success came to seem.

Each plot, he reasoned, ran some risk of failure. Given that, he thought the present plan at least as promising as any other; and given Stanley's lust, his excitement, perhaps more promising. Further, the plan was relatively simple to enact; and yet its effects were distant and convoluted and would be brought into play by the normal agents of retribution. Finally, he would be forced to enlist only one other wight in his aid. The one thing he did not fear was to be stopped by those agents himself—city, state, or federal. In part, his concentrated passion made dim or small of any problem but his immediate and direct dealing with his enemy. But implicitly, as well, it called into practice a principle handed down to him by one of the town's most eminent attorneys the summer before he entered law school. It was said that no one since Robert Frost had been so aptly named as Randolph Wright, Randy to friend and foe alike, a big bald florid man, wearing thick glasses and a white linen suit in need of a cleaning, for no one had a finer sense of the proper use to be made of the fairer sex no matter the age, shape, size, race, creed, color, or national origin, and no one had so fine a sense of the intricate weave, the delicate poise, the yin and yang, as it were, of right and wrong. Mr. Wright had felt called upon at that time, in the absence of the young man's father, to bestow on him an advice both paternal and professional. Just remember one thing, he had said, swaying like a mighty cobra preparing to strike his drink, any lawyer worth his stuff can do anything at all illegal on a few hours' notice and get away with it. Loren had waited respectfully then for the expected moral, the injunction of the holy order's high responsibility, that, given that ability, the lawyer worth his stuff must exercise self-restraint, must regulate himself in the interest of the law as concept, as ideal; but it had not come. Instead the great man had adduced the current example of incompetence: Take those little shits in the White House. They're all going to get caught because they ha'n't got it. Anyone can see that. Just a matter of time. They simply aren't worth their stuff, aren't up to the very crimes they had ever' right to commit. They aren't stupid after all; they got to protect themselves. But they ha'n't the guts to carry it through. That cynicism, the vivid hyperbole, the antiquated image of the leading citizen above the law, amused Loren; and early in his years at law school the phrase, *worth his stuff*, became, by repetitions of the story, the badge of dishonor affixed to those of their classmates who he and his friends were certain would become in time the lawyers' lawyers, salamanders, oiled and able to live in fire and water, the clones of Mr. Max Bunting. But he had learned since that time that the principle was a close approximation to the truth. There was very little a lawyer who set his mind to it, so long as he had the mind to set, could not do and make it appear all nice and legal or, better yet, like a magician, not make it appear at all. He knew, that is, that he could acquire as many counterfeit bills as he needed, with nothing lost but the going price for them. He knew further that he would get them without comment or question. That was just the way things stood between him and Hank Savich for services previously rendered, for Loren's extricating him from a marriage hastily contracted, contracted in despair after the death of his first wife, the long slow collapse under cancer, by the simple expedient of turning up the second wife's first husband, from whom she had never troubled herself, contemptuous of the law as she was, to become legally disjoined. He knew Hank had his ways of getting what he wanted. He knew that his beer distributorship did not thrive by Hank's industry alone and had tried not to listen too closely when his client had talked during that time of service rendered about his simply having the bitch put to sleep. Now there was need for the things Hank could do for him. It was that simple. The matter would be taken care of.

If the state were less reliable and less efficient than Hank Savich, Loren could feel relatively confident that one of its arms would carry out its duties and gain his revenge for him. There were problems of course: the state might not move quickly to apprehend him; apprehended, he would try to implicate the man who had duped him; he might recognize the money for what it was before the deal had been closed. But none seemed insuperable. The state might be encouraged by that honored practice, the anonymous tip. His word to the contrary was scarcely to be impugned by Stanley's ravings. He might finally not pay anything until he had all the evidence in hand and trust to the conditions surrounding the exchange—the dark of night, distractions, the carelessness imposed by haste, Stanley's excitement—to aid him. He would not pay anything that afternoon, that was it; he would run that risk, he would call Stanley's hand. But then he remained certain that the one thing Stanley wanted was the money and drew from that the conclusion that he would not do anything ultimately to end his chances of getting it. The longer he held the plan in mind, however, the less satisfied with it he became. He could argue either side of the case with conviction: it would work, it wouldn't; it posed this further risk; it lacked this essential property. His earlier excitement he knew to be a boy's glee; he had been monstrously foolish to waste his time on these futile schemes, these ruses doomed to failure. But now he had no choice. His sands ran out. He had to move quickly. It was ten-thirty. Perhaps modifications could be introduced later. But for the moment he had to act. Even at that his debtor whistled between his teeth and said that it might take more time to get together that many bills. Loren told him simply that he didn't think he had more time. Hank considered for a minute, then said that he would see what he could do, and hung up. At that Loren could relax a bit; at least that would be taken care of. What he could not accomplish as easily was to recover that zest which had covered his bitter indignation, his anger, his fear like a sugar coating. He had worn the coating off and was left with the medicine to swallow as he could. What, finally, he would not consider was to damn Stanley to his own devices and forget about it altogether.

He glanced quickly at his correspondence (Mr. Bamberger, who wanted to sue the Walker-Davis Company for polluting the stream which ran by his farm and poisoning his cows; the group bringing suit against his father's mills for his failure to provide a place to work free of hazard; Clarence Wilson, who asked for a report on progress in their negotiations with the North Carolina State Police to have a *DUI* charge—unseemly on a physician's record and bad for business—suppressed or reduced to a lesser offense tho they had him cold on the Breathalyzer test), set the letters aside, and called for Mrs. Portman. It was his routine to work alone and undisturbed through the early morning and for her to intercept his business calls and take messages, which she would then convey when he was ready for them. Occasionally she took it upon herself to interrupt him before he called for her, with the plea of grave importance or special dispensation, tho invariably the matter turned out to be not nearly so pressing as she had thought nor to require any handling out of the ordinary and he surmised that this was her means of establishing her own existence, the confirmation of a life's effort at it, at least one result of which had been to run her husband, a slight mild unassuming man who repaired watches for a living, off to Oregon with a spinster schoolteacher. Loren had learned all of this when he hired her, even the fact of the schoolteacher's first marriage, an impassioned fugue, years before, which her parents had had annulled; it had been the most painful interview of his life, a life which had constantly to hear the accounts of another's distress; but he had discerned in the woman, behind the self-importance, the presumption, a flinchless loyalty to anyone or anything who would simply declare himself or itself her master. She still waited for her husband to return, as soon, she said, as he came to his senses and grew tired of his hussy. That was scarcely the word to describe Miss Buckler, who Loren remembered from high school was enthralled to *Pride and Prejudice* and an avid fan of the sports played by adolescents. And he doubted that Mr. Portman would ever regain those lamented faculties.

The last message this morning was from a Mr. Sims; it confirmed their appointment for that afternoon.

"He wouldn't leave his number," Mrs. Portman said, puffing up her substantial bulk in a show of indignation, "and I don't have him on the calendar."

"It's all right," Loren said. "I know what it's about."

"Will you be going out or will he be coming in?" she inquired.

"I'll be going out," he said in a manner to which she had become accustomed and so which did not deter her.

"Should I draw up a contract for you to take with you?" she asked, pressing her luck.

"No, that won't be necessary."

Still she lingered. "I don't believe I know any Sims."

Loren offered an explanation. "It's a fairly large town, Mrs. Portman. If I didn't know you, I wouldn't know a Portman; and yet there must be a half dozen of them in the phone book."

"There are seven," she said. "None related. None to me at least."

"Well, there must be at least that many Sims."

"There are eleven. Not counting variations."

"Well, this is all very interesting, Mrs. Portman. But I'm sure you must have things to do."

Mrs. Portman could not encroach beyond a line so precisely drawn, so turned and bore her dignity off with the same unsuccess of a former movie queen in older age attempting to mount in public a vanished beauty, the difference being that, for all her virtues, she knew of dignity only what she had read in *Reader's Digest* on the subject. She had no sooner closed the door than the bulletin board which hung behind it received the letter opener, a heavy thin engraved brass blade, which Loren had picked up while they talked, balanced nervously, point and pommel between his palms, and then let fly in savage flight as soon as her back was turned and covered. The blade quivered where it stuck; the few memos which hung there rustled briefly, then fell still. Goddam him, was the sole message Loren could form; he repeated it, letting the words out like the air from a punctured tire. He had not counted on this; he feared the consequences of Stanley's calling Mrs. Portman, as it were, to witness their exchange, even if she stood at a distance and had no idea what she did. The woman would not forget that name; she lived on rumor and gossip; if just the hint of their misdealing reached her, she could now place them together for anyone who wished to listen. Whether she would speak what she knew was another matter. But Loren imagined that her silence would have its own high price: his suffering her to raise herself to conspiratress, the intimacy between those who share a secret. In this, however, he blamed his bad luck. He waved off the thought that Stanley was perhaps more cunning than he had at first believed. His enemy in his incontinence had, he thought, without knowing what he did, brought about exactly what Loren had wanted to prevent. Until this moment he had had only to worry that a chance passerby would recognize them in the park. But the pool was far from any road and of course deserted at that time of year, and his concern had not been great. They might be seen but, if they left by separate paths especially, would not be recognized.

But this: this threatened all, like opening the door to a dark room; it gave him something which he might sometime have to explain.

The message made him angry, but it did not make him careful (for one thing, there was little care to be taken: all that he could do he had done, all that he could do now was to await the appointed hour), nor did it cause him to revise his assessment of Stanley's aspirations, any more so than his abilities. He knew the man so well, forced, as he had been, into the close observation of him during the previous six months. He could not remember ever finding so little to approve or recommend in another human being; and to maintain a certain stability in his own mind, he had stripped Stanley of all things human, the mere vestiges of human emotions, had thrust him backward in the evolution of the species and made of him some gloomy hirsute atavism, an organism moved solely by unmitigated appetites. As evidence he had Stanley's declaring once, smiling complacently, that he despised rich people, not for principle or reasons of abstract justice nor for anything due him, but for the omission, that he was not among them, despised them for having the things he wanted. There are those moments when anyone is revealed in his purity, when the aleatory accretions are knocked off, when the defenses are down, when the concessions are too onerous to be made, when the inner self clamors to be revealed; and Loren thought that that was Stanley's moment. There, he thought thereafter, was the man, the manikin. And nothing he had learned since then had altered his understanding. A passion, a higher order process, a thought was simply beyond his means; he had so little concern for others that one might almost diagnose a lesion to that part of the brain which allows us to recognize them. In his own home he stood out, begrimed and unkempt, as if even there he had failed to adapt where everything favored him. Loren could only assume that that acceptance was the usual anomaly and owed something to a shared feeling among the members of the family similar to his own deference to Linda on the subject and perhaps to an embarrassed silence, brought on by disbelief and sustained by their powerlessness, similar to that which afflicted his victim when Stanley, it was rumored but never accurately stated nor proved, unzipped his pants and exposed himself to her in the deserted halls of the high school. The poor girl, just fifteen at the time, and three years younger than her assailant, had absolutely refused to see the principal to report the incident; her hysterics mounted at the suggestion that she describe what she had seen; and some of the boys had talked of taking matters into their own hands and meting out their own justice for the offense. But so far as Loren knew, nothing had ever come of that, and Stanley had gained another reason for doing as he pleased. Not only was there pleasure to be had but also there was no punishment to be feared among the consequences of his acts.

He had among other things, at this time, his sister's lover's apparently respectful ear while she got herself slowly ready for their quiet evenings out. Loren bore those conversations with the grace he had been reared to practice. But he had never managed to convince himself that Stanley was not so bad as all that after all. Stanley was that bad. His parents were not, and Loren found much to admire and like them for. But they, in their modesty, had little to say to him; and he, in his arrogance, his vast experience, his position, had as little to say to them. To Stanley he had as little to say or less and would have preferred to sit and watch television with her father until she was ready. But there he was, constantly pressing forward, asking advice, rendering opinions: the jew bankers in New York had caused the energy crisis by angering the Arabs; the niggers brought on the domestic turmoil by their claim of rights they did not deserve because they had not earned them; the government was run by jews and niggers, people who didn't work for a living themselves, who made their livings off the sweat of others, like himself. They were opinions with which Loren was already familiar, pieces of mind not uncommon among the set into which he had been born. But those of his set he met on even terms: he could despise them with good conscience and dispute their views as ardently as he wished. But in Stanley's parents' home he was a guest and felt acutely the obligations of a guest. He attributed a discomfort to them, similar to his own, which he would not aggravate by an objection too long or too loud. He made the best of their son he could. But the very imposition of silence angered him: that he should sit by and content himself with a modest mumbled emendation or clarification of that other's facts. It helped not at all that Stanley, tho not ugly, had made himself repulsive: dirt lay layers deep on his hands and forearms; he carried with him always, like an aura, the stale smell of oil and sweat and tobacco and bad breath; his lank hair clung like a leech to his head, oddly out of proportion with his strong simian body; he walked now with a limp he had furnished himself by cutting off one of his toes with an ax in order to avoid service in Vietnam.

Stanley was that bad and got worse with age, with knowing him. He made a show of courting Loren's confidence; he gave rise to doubts; he presented the evidence which his parents apparently could deny but which Loren could not—the cameras, radios, cassette tape decks, the pocket calculators, the dictaphones, the jewels, the odd pieces of silver—little of which alone, much less together, could he have afforded to purchase on his salary. There was challenge, defiance, in the display, piece by piece, in, as it turned out, his fascinated discourse on the working of the electronic equipment, his delighted exclamation on the ease with which one could record another's words without his knowledge, as there was in his various acts of hospitality. He seemed to dare Loren to call him on it, to ask once where this or that had come from. He dared Loren to call him before his parents what he had made bold repeatedly to prove himself. He dared and Loren did not take it. Instead he murmured platitudes on the weather and the conditions of the country and longed for Linda to be ready on time for a change. But when he brought the fact to her attention and gently urged her not to leave him sitting there alone, she replied ingenuously that her mother was so pleased to have him in the house. She thinks you're so good-looking, Linda replied, and she appreciates the interest you take in Stanley, listening to him and all. She's always been afraid for Stanley, always afraid he wasn't quite right in the head, you know. She thinks it's good for him to talk to you. She keeps wanting him to take courses at the junior college like I did. I don't think he'll ever do it, do you? I don't know, Loren said, he seems to have other things to do with his nights. Her silence had made him think that perhaps she was not so ingenuous as she seemed.

It went almost without saying that one thing Stanley did not do with his nights was love. He had once laid bare his heart to his unwilling confidant, having first declared that he would know what he was talking about. It seemed, Stanley had said, that he could only get it on with whores; he had suspected in passing that his problem was another legacy of Army life, but that was only the circumstance. He had affected worry: he wanted a child as much as the next man; he had tried to like normal women but had always come away from the encounters deeply dissatisfied; but he couldn't, could he, be expected to marry a whore. The conversation had taken place many weeks before, in midsummer, as they stood together in the front yard, waiting. It was twilight, and the lightning bugs had begun their languid rise like the bubbles in a glass of warm champagne. The heat of day had subsided, and with its going a quiet, broken by the shouts of children running free after supper, had settled on the neighborhood. Sprinklers sent sprays of water onto several of the lawns, each lawn small and square and threadbare even with the watering before each house small and square and distinguished from its neighbor by the paint on its shingles. What do you think? Stanley had insisted on knowing. What do you mean? Why do you ask me? Loren had said to hold him off. Aw c'm'on, Loren. I know you better'n that, he had said, laughing. And you know me. W'y, we're as like as two peas in a pod. W'y, we're just like brothers. There's nothing we don't know about each other or could not understand. So that was it, Loren had thought. He had not been trying to insinuate himself by all this talk into my good graces but by that emphasizing our differences and making known to me who already know it and to him who wants to forget it how far apart we will always be, but rather by all this talk to reveal how similar we are especially to me who would deny it. And only Linda's calling that she was ready had saved him from making the answer he had wanted to make and from delivering the blow he had wanted badly to deliver. What were y'all talking about? she had wanted to know. He had managed a bleak smile which passed unnoticed in the twilight. He wanted to know if my intentions in regard to you were honorable. She had had at least the good sense to laugh. Oh Stanley. He wouldn't know it if he saw it, so has no way of knowing if what you told him was the truth.

Oh. Her good sense covered more ground than that.

And she seemed in general to harbor no illusion about her brother tho she rarely spoke about him and then only in passing. Her reticence in itself was evidence of something, for the chronicle of her family—her parents, aunts, uncles, cousins, her sister Janey and her husband and their child—was her first order of conversation; and he inferred that Stanley had somehow violated her sense of family to be so consistently denied the place which natural law had made for him. Loren wondered now what his enemy had done to efface himself, as it were, from the happy *genre* scenes—the picnics, the Christmas parties, the leave-takings, the returns, the disagreements so that the reconciliations were the sweeter—which she painted for him. He was not completely effaced: he was rather a smudge, a shadow, a skull, an incongruous detail left in the corner where it sat in the normal course of things by the painter to baffle her critics with, whether she had intended an ironical statement on the happy home by that inclusion or whether her sense of realism had been such that she had simply put everything down in its place without discrimination or comment. Loren did not know and he wondered now what else had not passed between them. To this time little else had seemed important but the moments they lived; and he had no more regarded the past, even that that she thrust upon him by her talk, than he had the future, on which she also was silent. But now he wondered; in his distress and uncertainty he counted what he did know, like a miser his gold, able only to trust that which he could array in stacks before him: her lithe delicate body, the curl of her hair, the convolutions of her ear, the frankness of her eyes; her taste in music, which he had enriched; the books she read, because he chose them for her; her refusal to be put down or to put another down if she could help it; her appreciation of the things done for her; her unfailing willingness to ascribe the best of motives to her friends, acquaintances, and associates; her devotion to the man she gave her heart to and her reluctance to ask for it back tho, or when, he proved unequal to the care it required; her general enthusiasm, which nevertheless never seemed to wear thin; her eagerness to learn; her unashamed desire for the satisfactions of flesh and spirit. She seemed perfect in her small way: a lovely intricately carved figure in ivory, three inches tall; saddened rather than irritated when things did not go her way; given to moods which did not endure; forgiving and if possible forgetful. But just by thinking of her in this way, he knew he had transformed her and himself, made them both a pair of objects, himself the matching piece perhaps and exquisitely done but cold and void and incomplete as a fossil. He hated himself for it, but could not change it. And when his private telephone rang again, he stopped himself from reaching for it. She would be his caller, and he could not speak to her just yet. He had to think, to decide, to reach some conclusions. The instrument rang insistently a half-dozen times and then fell silent, leaving the room quieter and more ominous than it had found it, poised and expectant. That tension was broken almost immediately by the ringing of his office telephone, which he cursed even as he took it up. Mrs. Portman informed him that his mother wanted to talk to him.

Her voice had the shadings of her momentary unease. "Loren? I just called your private line."

He saw no reason to keep the truth from her. "I just let it ring. I thought it might be someone else."

Whether that satisfied her or not, she did concede his prerogative. "Well, it's your own life, and I won't interfere. Mrs. Portman says you haven't been out of the office all morning."

He answered curtly. "It's turned out to be busier than I expected."

She made her own interpretation of that information. "I suppose you're just saying that to give yourself an excuse for missing my meeting this afternoon. Your friend Max Bunting is coming up from Columbia."

Loren felt the need to correct her. "Max doesn't have friends, Mama. For that matter I don't think he has enemies. There are two categories of people in his life—victims and potential victims. A few people, like his wife and children, are in both categories simultaneously."

She scoffed, "Oh Loren. I do think you exaggerate."

He rejoined, with little interest, "There's no point in exaggerating. The truth is bad enough. If you don't believe me, ask Rita Lazarus what Harold thinks about him."

Having already asked Mrs. Lazarus and received her

usual evasive reply, Mrs. Owings began, "It's not that I don't believe you—"

And invited her son's interruption, "What time is it?"

Encouraged, she said promptly, "They'll be here around three."

He paused, as if making calculations, and then gave her the answer she expected. "Mama, I've really too much to do today."

Even so, and to establish a future credit, she coaxed, "Oh Loren, I had so counted on you to help us persuade this young man."

He was quick to answer this time. "Well, if that's all, I'm saved. I doubt seriously that Max would really listen to anything I had to say. And I do have a lot to do."

She all but sighed. "Well, if that's the way it is, I shan't press you on it. Will you be coming home to supper?"

So it goes, he thought, this for that; then said, "Yes, I'll be there. I might have to go out again. But I'll be there then."

She said slyly, "Is it that young woman again?"

Chilled, in rather too much haste, he asked, "What young woman?"

She answered blandly, "Why, that young woman you've not introduced your family to. Isn't there always a young woman?"

Wondering whether he should feel relief, he said, "I don't know what you are talking about."

She would not let him get away so easily. "Don't

you? She's blonde, isn't she? Petite, with blue eyes? And apparently, altogether too good for your own family."

He called her bluff. "I didn't think you'd appreciate the fact that she's a Hollins girl."

She rewarded him with a laugh; and before she could make another comment, he said, "Now I really must go. Have a good meeting. And don't forget about Max and the silver."

She laughed again and they bade each other farewell, and it was only after he had laid the receiver down with a trembling hand that he could count the cost to him of holding in place that ordinary mask. It seemed made of lead. He felt exhausted, the bubbling popping well of anger run dry; and he considered the notion, for several moments, of refusing flatly to be blackmailed and daring Stanley, in his turn, to do what he could or wanted with the photographs. Why not? he posed out of his dejection. Why in God's name not? He had not asked that these demands be made of him; he had not willingly accepted that, as his mother had often repeated throughout his childhood and adolescence, much was expected of him because much had been given him. Oh, he did agree, did accept. He had been blessed and he took it upon himself to bless in return. But he wanted to do so in his own manner, at his own speed, and without the pressure of an extortion behind him. All right, he would say, the advantages have been mine, but let me correct the balance as I see fit. That, however, he had always felt, was the license the world was not willing to grant. They wanted constantly to know what he was doing, it seemed. His social and athletic exploits as a student, his professional and disguised political activities as an adult, his present standing as the community's most eligible bachelor, all were matters others than himself had deemed fit for public scrutiny. A week did not pass but that his name appeared conspicuously in the local newspaper: Loren Owings this, Loren Owings that. He hated that constant nagging, that constant boring into his skin, tho there seemed no way for him to stop it. It crossed his mind that here perhaps was that way he had never found. If they wanted something so badly, then let them have something really to astonish them: not another donation, not another public statement, but the incontrovertible evidence of dishonor and disrepute. They would not know that the dishonor was theirs for their prurience, but he did not care. It mattered only at that moment that he be left in peace.

He knew, however, that for some time to come he would find no peace: no quiet of spirit, no ease of flesh. He wanted sleep, having slept scarcely at all and that the languid possessed sleep between consummations and before the violation and his rage and the need to comfort her made sleep impossible; he wanted sleep to forget if possible and if not to oil the workings of his mind, to stop the screaming and grinding of the mechanisms. He knew that, until he found some relief, his ability to decide anything would be gravely impaired, and with the desperation of a drowning man clutching at a straw he shook two aspirin tablets from the plastic container he kept in his desk. He could not risk anything stronger, neither to relax nor to stimulate him; he could not sleep, so needful was he to maintain appearances, so much had he to do. The white tablets nestled in his palm like eggs: their whiteness, their delicately suspended friability frightened him. He saw his life in the two tablets: unstable, at risk constantly, soon to dissolve, to break and splinter and disperse. Jesus, he thought angrily, the waste, the goddam waste; then popped the tablets into his mouth and forced them down with a swallow of the cold stagnant coffee still patiently standing by on his desk. Relief was very slow to arrive, and at noon he found himself still prey to the pain, still staring past the wide rosewood desk, past the Barcelona chairs across from him, to the far wall of his office, where hung the reproduction of one of Georgia O'Keeffe's paintings, the bleached skull of a cow, a desert stillness.

At that hour his partner and their three associates entered his office. They led Mrs. Portman pushing a tea wagon on which she had arranged sandwiches, potato chips in cellophane bags, and soft drinks, delivered from the coffee shop downstairs, and a carrot cake which she had baked. So commenced, as usual, their weekly congregation, at which time the general policy of the firm was discussed and established and the members' specific problems were presented and dealt with. The meeting kept them all abreast and, Loren knew, gave them the look of a solid front as they competed for new clients, clients, that is, since there was no dearth of souls passionately desiring to sue someone or something else, of a certain order. He thought that apparent unity important to their success; and tho he little doubted their becoming eventually a firm of standing, he knew that his fellows expected that to be attained sooner rather than later and so adopted any strategy which promised to hasten them onto the pedestal. They deserved to be there, it was already said. They were by and large a fine collection of young men and without question a fine collection of attorneys, and under normal circumstances, at this moment, Loren allowed himself the luxury of the pleasant memory that older and established firms throughout the state had wanted them badly, tho they all but denied it now, but that he, by employing the only counterweight to their arguments of reputation that he had—his family's money—had managed to sign them on when three years after leaving law school himself he had gone out, as the saying is, on his own. They were extremely well paid; they had the prospect of early advancement; none was expected, for the firm's or the public's good, to serve a term or two in the state legislature, to play politics where one's chances of success were significantly diminished. The money, the privileges he accorded, the promises he extended had at least brought good weight—too good in fact for his present comfort. They were discerning, perspicacious, skilled in the traffic of cues, signs, symbols; and Loren had the feeling, from the moment they entered the office, that, intrigued, a bit puzzled perhaps, they were watching him very closely. He kept therefore to himself, so much as possible, leaning back in the leather chair behind his desk, having first drawn out one of its lower drawers to rest his well-shod foot upon, listening to the others for slips of tongue or innuendos which might give them away, his head slightly bowed, his eyes peering steadily forward, one arm folded across his chest and supporting the other arm, which held its hand in place, discreetly hiding his lips.

When in due course the meeting broke up, his partner, John Abruzzi, the son of an Italian grocer in Brooklyn, who had come south to play defensive back for the university football team and then had stayed to settle, lingered, hands in pockets, the features of his coarse dark appealing face suitably composed. It was not unusual for them to carry on after the others left, to speak their minds with a bit more candor on the subjects of mutual interest, to assess their colleagues' abilities, and generally to congratulate themselves on their success. Still, Loren knew this answered no ordinary purpose and expected his friend to ask casually if there were something wrong and so had his answer ready, so ready in fact that it fairly burst off his tongue. "No. I'm just a little tired, I guess."

Then, fearing that that might cause suspicion, he added, mustering a wan smile, "Maybe I've been working too hard."

"What the hell, Loren," his partner said, permitting himself to be taken in, "that's what we hired them for, to do the work. Why don't you take it easy?"

Then he laughed and followed them, their associates, from the office. At the door, however, he all but paused, all but reached for the embedded letter opener, a set of movements so quick, so subtle that

Loren would not have noticed them had he not been watching for them, watching anxiously for just this confirmation that he had been found out. All right, he thought; so you know. I can't do anything about that now. John slowed his pace but did not pause, moved his hand impulsively but did not reach, then passed on without turning his head or speaking. The door closed silently behind him. So, you too I have to worry about, thought Loren ruefully; you too have something to contribute when time comes to explain the victim's disintegration and something to atone for, that you didn't, couldn't, wouldn't help, couldn't.

The lode of his affection for his partner was far too rich for him to feel at this time that he had somehow been betrayed. He reminded himself that just this quality of discernment, of deep and uncanny sensibility, had been the personal attribute which had first attracted him to the man and that he could scarcely expect that sense in another to fail because it suited him. He considered it still his greatest coup that he had been able to lure John into the risky partnership. No one, even in an age given to excessive praise, had ever made John out to be better than a competent attorney, tho no one equally denied that he was surely that. What he had done, however, what he had brought with him when he came, what he had added to the enterprise, what made him still so terribly important, more so even than his kind of acuity, was color, dash, panache, the raw plumage to distinguish them from the other birds in the legal forest. There was scarcely to be found a man of a certain age in the state, that critical age among businessmen when it fell to them to decide which law firm to hire, who did not recall Abruzzi's punt return, in the final minutes, to upset the previously undefeated and eighth-ranked Georgia Bulldogs. He had taken the ball over his shoulder as it bounced toward the coffin corner, a defensive strategy intended to pin the Gamecocks hopelessly in their own territory for the duration (and to extricate the Bulldogs from a game they had expected to win easily), had turned, twisted, fought off the first tacklers, picked up his blockers, and by midfield had sprung free, to be carried home upon the waves of sound, the disbelieving, joyous, primitive sound of those true believers in delirium. The old athletic offices at the university has displayed for years a photograph of the young man eluding the last desperate Georgia player; and once Loren, half in earnest, had suggested that they ought to get an enlarged copy of that photograph for the wall of the reception area in their law offices. John had demurred: Hell Loren. No one cares about that anymore. Just so we win for them now. What we really ought to get is a couple of Jasper Johns. Now that would be impressive. Of course he had been wrong about the photograph; of course he was right about the Johns. They were impressive, in stark contrast to the refurbished paneling of the room, the self-consciously clubby look; and almost invariably they evoked comment from a client visiting the offices for the first or second time and, occasionally, when he thought about it, Loren's amusement at the imagined dealings between his friend, the mountain peasant, and the patrician banker, Leo Castelli, for those prized objects they both loved. His error, his showing wrong on whether people still cared about his exploit, was revealed in the fact that he had been raised from the good player that he was to the best ever to play the position for the university to finally the equal of the great Scott of Georgia, who succeeded him by a full decade. He had been wrong and Loren right—it was that simple. And if he preferred to talk about the Johns and the Warhols, on which he had his eye but at which Loren still drew the line ("At least we can say, if it comes to it, that Johns is a native son. What can we say at all about Warhol? He doesn't come from anywhere. He comes from outer space."), he could and would talk football for hours and in ten minutes within that time assure his interlocutor that of course they would take the man's problems for their own. He knew people, as the saying is, knew instinctively the gum and baling wire which held them together, and even so liked them; and when the gum and baling wire failed, he had sympathy for them. His wife Cheryl had imposed one condition before the partnership could be formed and sealed. I want you to promise me one thing, Loren, she had said. I don't want you to take on any homeless clients. We've got enough mouths to feed around here without John bringing home another.

He had kept his promise to Cheryl Abruzzi (tho she herself had broken it recently by giving birth at thirty-eight to their sixth child, a sturdy little boy with curly hair, whom they loved dearly) and together they prepared to prosper a bit sooner than even he had dared to hope. But now, as he left the offices, he had the distinct and unpleasant sense, as of a patient gravely ill, made to breathe, eat, and evacuate by a reticulation of plastic tubes, that he was to lose this place, never to see it again, that he was to become, furthermore, that burden to his associates which he had promised her never, never to take on. That sadness and five thousand dollars in counterfeit bills, which Hank had sent over in a brown paper wrapper, were what he took with him when he left the offices at three-forty. The bills made ugly uncomfortable lumps in the pockets of his coat; but he did not want to carry his briefcase, even for the benefit of Mrs. Portman, who regarded him with close suspicion as he passed her without speaking. The city park was less than a mile from his offices; but because he wanted to be first on the scene, he took his car from the lot, with some regret that he hadn't anticipated this necessity and driven to work in the sedate and indistinguishable Buick rather than his secret pride and joy, the red Porsche. He stopped himself from taking this too as an omen, the prediction clear and simple that his plans were to collapse like a house of cards and with them the life he had chosen to live, leaving him a legend in his own time, broken, mad, a burden to his kind, a bogeyman, inhabiting the basement of the family mansion and employed by mothers in their stories to frighten their young children into obedience and eventually himself pestered by those same children grown to adolescence and no longer quite so willing to believe in ghosts.

The park was an irregularly shaped plot of ground, bounded on one side by a pond of even more irregular shape, the waters of which seemed always to be a light orange-brown in color; together land and water claimed perhaps thirty acres. At one time in the city's history, a zoo had stood upon one corner of the grounds, tho zoo is perhaps too fine a name for the sad collection of fauna—deer and raccoon and opossum—which it sheltered. But now the only animals in residence were the squirrels and chipmunks which ran free and the white ducks released to their own devices from the desperate care of children six months after Easter. The old tennis courts had been paved with asphalt and furnished with lights; the city pool had become the domain, in summer, of the usual assortment of scream-ing laughing black children. At this time of year, at this time of day, the park was deserted, the courts were not in use, and the pool, painted its peculiar shade of aquamarine, was empty and beginning to collect dead leaves and broken twigs in the dry corners. As he walked purposefully across the leafy hollow which formed the park, Loren descried Stanley, his back to-ward him, perhaps one hundred yards away. He would not then have the advantage, that small advantage of being first on the ground; but charged with the strong desire to have something, to regain something, any-thing, even just to startle his enemy by his silent ap-proach, he quickened his pace. Even that small antic-ipated pleasure, however, was denied him. Stanley slowly, continuously rotated in place and came pres-ently to face his victim while he was still some forty yards away. They did not gesture to each other but even at that distance Loren could see that Stanley grinned happily, as his hands, which had been hanging loose, moved to the side pockets of his jacket. Without thinking Loren imitated the movement, patted the pockets where he kept the stacks of bills. When they were close enough to speak, Stanley said, "Well, Loren. This is a surprise."

Loren spoke rapidly and, after the first glimpse of his antagonist's face, without looking at him directly: "You go to hell. Now let's step aside some place."

Stanley's ebullience was not to be denied. "No, no, Loren. This place suits me fine. Say, you don't look so good. You don't look any better than you sound."

"Leave it, Stanley. Let's just get this over with."

Stanley pretended offense. "Now wait a minute. Not so fast there, Loren. I want this to be all on the up and up. Did you bring the money, first?"

Loren was at pains to keep from becoming sick to his stomach. He could feel Stanley's eyes on him, the polluted eyes, as repulsive as his perpetually dirty fingers; they stared at him with such a happy intensity that they pressed upon his skin. And in consequence he felt himself beginning to collapse. "Yes. Did you bring the pictures?"

"Of course, my friend, of course. What do you take me for? I brought the one picture now. And I brought Xerox copies of the other two, just so's you'll know what you're getting later on. Here, le'me show you."

Loren murmured, disheartened, "It doesn't matter."

But Stanley would not relent. "No. I want to. Here."

No preparation, no urging of caution, would have sufficed to keep Loren from gasping when he looked quickly at the grainy copies Stanley thrust upon him. The remaining heart went out of him in that gasp. He felt a numbness, a rubberiness to his being, which he had only felt before when his lips, under his mother's duress, as she broke down finally ("Oh please, Loren, for me. Kiss your father good-bye"), touched the cheek of his father's body as it lay in the coffin. His father's cheek had had that same quality and had imparted it to him at that moment. The photographs were appalling, ugly, brutal: violation beyond the scope of violation, a desecration of what had always been to him the entirely beautiful. These were not of the love he knew. But in his anger, his despair, they came to represent and mean and finally, with alarming speed, be the love. He clung to the love he knew but felt it run through his fingers. And he was left with the foul residue, the glossy paper, the spots, the stains, and the conviction that he would never again be able to submit himself to that grotesque ritual. Pity stirred in his mind, a pity similar to that he felt when presented with scenes of the victims of war, hunger, natural disaster: the poor souls battered, broken by circumstances over which they themselves had no control. There they were, strangers to him, himself a stranger to him, twisted, exposed, despised. There was no beauty in them; they were horrible, as horrible as death. He felt dead and embalmed. He opened his mouth to speak, but no words came from him.

"Lovely, ain't they?" Stanley inquired, sniggering.

"You pig," gasped Loren, in the manner of an echo, the sound of an empty bottle when one blows across the mouth. "You disgusting pig."

Stanley gleamed. "Now just hold on there. You want 'em back or don't you? I ain't give 'em back yet. I've still got 'em. The real you. Heh, heh."

Loren gasped. "Give them to me. Now."

Stanley played it out with high seriousness, in strict form. "No, Loren. We got a deal. One now, as soon as you give me the money. The rest tonight, at that ol' church your mama seems so proud of. Let's make it ten o'clock. That'll give us plenty of time. Now the five thousand."

As if in a dream, Loren handed over the money and received the original photograph; he barely noticed or acknowledged the exchange or the instructions for their second meeting.

"And don't forget to bring your sister," Stanley said, continuing to snigger.

Shaken, restored to his senses, Loren exclaimed, "My sister!"

"Shore, didn't I tell you? Now that was clumsy of me. Shore, the twenty thousand is for your good name, and cheap at that, I might say. Your sister is for my trouble. It's only fair, ain't it? You roll mine. I roll yours. Turn about's fair play. That's what I always say."

He had, however, barely time to say it. The raw swirling elements of Loren's disintegration, galvanized by those appalling words, suddenly coalesced. And fast as lightning and with less warning, he drove his fist into Stanley's face, drawing blood from nose and lip and dropping him to the ground. Standing over the fallen man, he sought painfully for expression, "Ah, ah, I', I'." But his eyes at last found their mark. His gaze met Stanley's and held it; an intimacy almost of lovers flashed between them.

"W'y shore, shore. You do that," Stanley panted, sitting awkwardly where he had fallen and still remarkably unaware of what was to befall him yet. "You do that. But you be shore to bring your sister and the money with you tonight."

Loren trembled. His face was horribly twisted. But he had found what he wanted to say. "I'll kill you, you son of a bitch. I'll kill you."

Sobered, but unrepentant and unafraid, improbably brave and plumblessly foolish, Stanley spoke in a strangely soothing voice. "W'y shore, you do that. But I'll go out rich. And the mortician won't ever get the smile off my face."

# 4

Get out. Get away. What. Where. Find the car. All right, all right. I must stop this, must stop and get this together, I must. What. What is it. Shouts. Are they after me. Who. Children at play. Shouts from nowhere. Recapitulation. Anticipation. Did anyone see. Arrested for the destined crime before committed. Preventive medicine. Take your medicine. Take the will for the deed. How familiar, how inevitable. A boiling pot: the ingestion and regurgitation of ingredients, the constant turning over and over. Hermaphrodite. Her body. Breast. Thigh. Whose is whose. Stop. Dear God. Must think. No. Mustn't think. Some things are better hid forever. Some things hid forever. The sludge at the bottom of the sea, the most violent sea making indiscriminate claim of innocent and pirate, never tiring in its rage. The slow purposeful descent through black waters. Sleep. Susan. Dear God, no, what am I thinking. I must think, must plan. No time for sleep, for anything. Think. Wa. Wa. What. What. How. How am I to kill the son of a bitch. No delicacy now, no intricacy of plan. Just kill the son of a bitch. Too little time. A manipulation. Task in time. Problem solving. Simple: to eliminate a shadow, eclipse the sun. So much for God the son. Oh God. I must stop this. Think. Fragments. Ruins of thought. One thought only. Kill the son of a bitch. Kill the son of a bitch. Stop. No. Think. Slow down. Slow down and live. Alive and well at fifty-five. Where. Where am I. I can't believe. Start from the beginning. Where am I. Bermuda Triangle. The place ruled by Calibans. A city park. We never played here as children. Too far from our home. Other parks to play in closer by. The matter of several miles, a universe for children: their insularity, their small imaginations, the source of their matchless cruelty; how we thought the children who lived here, played here, were little monsters, the evil ones across town, the other side of the tracks. We never outgrow it, gain experience, activate imagination. The Arabs, the Chinese. The domain widens, but the suspicion, the fear of strangers, the fear of fear, the fear of ourselves, persists. Irony. The park is inhabited by monsters after all. Prescience. Vile creature. Snake which has deluded his own destiny and walks erect like a man. Homo erectus. But not me; the son of a bitch has not deceived me. I in fact have deceived him, it seems. Fool. He has placed his fate in my hands, without knowing what he's done.

Fool. He thinks he's won. He thinks he has me by the shorts. But I'll show him. Surprise him. Myself. I can. He has underestimated me. He doesn't think I can do it. He doesn't think I'm capable of it. The distinguished thing. Primal fear or modern refinement. He thinks I won't, can't. But he is wrong. I would. I will. After all, why not. Needless sentimentality about human life. We are what we eat. At play in our own excrement. Horrible has its fascination. So why not. Nothing human. What is it. *Nihil humani* something something. Mind full of holes. Sieve. Doesn't matter now. No mind at work or play. None needed. Reflex. The grasp to save oneself. My thing. Like the Great Wallenda falling to his death holding fast to his balance pole. That illusion of stability. Something to hold to. This will be easy, as easy and inevitable as a fall. The bastard. I do the world a service. The bloody minded bastard. Think. Things were so fine, would have been fine still. No. Wait. A term to all things. The limits of being. But not this, not like this. The secret. I was so close. That. That. Or this. This and that. The startling possibility, altering every previous conception. Yin and yang. Yes. We loved. But can anything so fragile withstand so vigorous an attack. The son of a bitch. His vileness. He doesn't know what he's done. It. It would just have gone on. Could just. Might just. All torn. That leer. No. Saw nothing. The terrifying whiteness. A polar field. Heard. That was it. That contemptuous laugh, respectless, unrepentant, resentful. Knew and didn't know at all. How could I not have heard something. The door catch disengaging, the shutter button. Something. Some warning. But nothing. The whiteness out of the blackness. Twice. Thrice. The ultimate denial. He could not know what he did. But for him it would have made no difference. That makes it easy. Doesn't it. The elimination of waste. The waste. I could do it for her as much as for myself. More. Will she ever love again without fear. O God. My sweet. My precious. I don't know. She is. She is. I gave up long ago trying to figure her out. She's amazed me always. What she would do or say or opine next. That freedom to tempt and challenge my constant probability. What I am. The poorly formed. The incomplete. A walking ruin. Do I love her. Could I. The words have been easy because everything about us has been easy. So little expected of me. For once. Just be. I don't know. Love myself as I am with her. Is that love. Nor do I know if she loves me. Don't know what love is. Abiding care, concern. A passionate pleasure in the other's triumphs. A willed fidelity. Whatever it is one's devotion measures. Whatever, when in any way denied, causes pangs of guilt. My guilt. That I could not marry her and her acceptance of that, blindly and without rebellion or complaint, as blindly as I did. What did I hide. What did I fear. This catatonic fit. This pose. What. To love them only to abandon them. To love them in order to abandon them. Why not love better or why love at all. Stanley's assessment. Alike as two peas in a pod. Closer to the truth than he imagined. Make whores of them all. The spiteful creatures. Love only. No. I must sustain it now. Must make it up to her. Time. What could a woman do which she has not done without my asking. There must be something wrong. There must be something to complain of. To give herself without losing herself. Freely. Trusting. Asking only a similar consideration. We are different, she said. Anyone can see that. We can't be the same. You're a man and I'm a woman. I don't mind. I like it this way. Our ups and downs. The joy. The slow crawl to understanding. Amazing. Just amazing. But to what end. What did we reach for. For this time. For this moment. For each other. And I the one obsessed with time. I could never give you a child. It's OK. But I think it's a shame because I think you'd make a good father. You're so good to me. But I guess I'll just have to find someone else to marry. But not to worry, she told me. She would always love me. Just like that. No apology. No recrimination. As if I were the injured one, the one to be consoled. Her astonishing pragmatism. And I said I wished I could do something for her, something to prove my love. And she asked did I want to pimp for her, did I not think she could do for herself whatever needed doing in the way of finding a man. No, I said, confused, embarrassed. I know, she said. You want to be able to do something. You feel guilty for this and want to make it up to me. But you don't have to. I forgive you everything. Everything. What kind of love permits this kind of talk between lovers. Who were we. Has she ever felt jealousy, betrayal, unfulfillment, dissatisfaction. Have I. What kind of love is it that does not admit these things. Maybe no love at all. No human enterprise. Did not love after all. The keen pleasure but nothing more, the more because there was nothing to betray, no deep commitment but to the moment, no future. Timeless. Out of time. Eternal for the moment. How little future there always was for us. An accumulation of smooth lustrous moments. Pearls on a string. The persistence, the confidence, the conviction of her own innocence so that even her former lovers she could talk about as if those experiences had happened to another person in another world and she reported only what she had heard. The season in Eden. One woman. One man. A time before time. The world within the world. The archetypes. No history. No future. I still don't understand. Her happy self-assertion. Well, I'm not perfect, but neither is anyone else and I've less to apologize for than most. Taking life as it comes. Making the most of it. But. But. Resignation but without submission. But something lost because something simply not gained. Achieved. Where did we go wrong. Where the apple. Where the brash copping of the forbidden fruit. Condemned after the fact. Not possible to be so happy. Were we. Cannot remember now. All so strange. Still no love without commitment. No guilt without history. Love more than love, being out of time. Now time. Stanley has destroyed it. I don't think she was capable of thinking there was such a thing as evil personified before this. The sweet encompassing illusion. Assumes some unrevealed purpose in the ways of the world. God's will. No accident in this. No random event. The hand of God. A test of her faith. Job's patience. Temptation to unbelief. Infidelity. No. She has mastered it. She will struggle along. Has mastered the form: churchgoing, genuflecting. No. I doubt it. She wouldn't see the utility of that. Everything its function. And where's the use of that. She would want to know. Where. Almost stamps her foot with her impatience to be answered. A feisty little creature not to be taken lightly. That indomitable spirit. Could she. Nothing to lose. Could I. Less. Yes. That spirit. That fire. The efflorescence. The fire in her appealing to the fire in me. Could we. Yes. The more she does, the more she can do. The limits of being far beyond what we have seen or done. Love giving birth to love. Yes. I have nothing to complain of. How many men might she love. Each as she could. Each as he required. Me. What I require. The horror. Man and manikin. Image and reality. Own dark places. Oppose them. Oppose myself. She feared nothing. Do with me what you will. Trust. Knew we would not ask too much. Restraint. Her needs, hopes, fears. My own. Would not abuse myself. The onanist. Do what you will. What do you want done. Pleasure. Nothing more. Blessing to give and to receive. Your own God. Blessed are the piece-makers, for they shall be called the children of God. Her laughter. She knew. Knew and approved. Whatever I wanted. Whatever she had to give. What do I want. What. Her boundless bounty. Everything. Everything a man could want. A woman whose benignant passions match his own. A mind to nurture. Ah that. Pygmalion, the master. No. I was the one enthralled.

By gaining everything. A peculiar slavery. And now the golden braids struck off. What. Old mad blind despised and dying. Mad George. Noble Lear. Nothing. Nothing. The earth rumbles and shakes, the present structures crack and collapse. Eruption. The hot wind. The rain of fire. Then things go deathly still. The cooling rubble. The ash in heaps. Defoliated trees standing like matchsticks or arrayed like rays emanating from the center of the blast. No. This is something different. Nuclear holocaust. Irradiation. The rain in Spain. Three people only, only two of whom will survive, and they, they as mutants. Refugees from the primeval swamp. Brave new world. Vacuum. Thoughts rushing to fill the vacuum. Life will out. Inexterminable cockroaches. A life not fit to live. Could we. Yes. Bear our love with us like the first amphibian its gills. Yes. She can do anything. Survive. With dignity. A force as elemental and enduring as the evil which opposes us. Will not ask. Will not need answers. Ask nothing of her men. No regrets. For love. Nor take from them anything but the pleasure and the sustaining memory. We loved once. It did work for a while. She is not heartless. She has suffered. Seen her suffering and perhaps have caused some, having missed my way, forgotten my place, misconstrued the obvious. But she has always gone on. It goes like it goes. Not me. Never. We are not the question. We could. We could. It's he. Who. Not whether we will survive but whether he will. Changed. All changed. I feel. What new thing. No. The everlasting no. The plates within shift and knock against each other. The eruption gathers. The fire within. *Cerveau plein de flamme.* Shifting plates. Altered schemas. Dislocation. Displacement. Dis. Disc. The big red disk. The sun. Hallu. Hallululation. I go mad. I know. I know. Hold on. Hold on to something. The Great Wallenda falling with his pole. The car. Where is the damn car. I must be calm. I must think. I must be calm. Where is the damn car. Where the hell am I. The hell am I.

The skuffling of the first fallen leaves. How I loved this as a child when I would help Odell with the raking. Shouts. Laughter. Getting in his way more than anything else. Odell. Who would not permit himself to be insulted. Or no longer. Even by a guest. Just fed up with it. Enough is enough. Too much. So quit. In the middle of a party. Set the silver tray of drinks down, they tell me, and walked out without a word of explanation. Mama never knew at least. A mystery to her still. And Ernest never told what he knew. Maybe he didn't know any better than we did. Didn't want to know. Those things we fear. The sudden disruption of whatever order there is. The cataclysm. The one bold stroke. Or so it seems. Given time, heart and mind will accommodate themselves to anything. Not so bad. Not so bad as all that, as I had feared. The sudden stroke is the devastating blow. No ablution for the old self now dead. Wanders in limbo, begging to be forgiven, pleading to be told what he had done, waiting to be ransomed by the living. Out of the blue. Or so it seems. But something must have gathered. Accumulated.

Nothing comes from nothing. No flame without a fuel. The little pains my father failed to register; the numbness, the tingling. And we, I had nothing to prepare me. What we don't know won't hurt us. And Odell's store of insults, until one further one brought about the explosion, the smoke, the smell, as our chemistry professor used to perform the last day of the course, combining innocent colorless liquids. Wild cheers. Laughter. Odell moved to Washington, we learned. The black Mecca. The end of that, so much as we were concerned, tho we often wondered among ourselves what had brought it about, what had happened, what was to become of him, as if he could not live without us. How nice to dispense with everything so easily. My father's death. Another matter altogether. Stanley. What motives, what imagined insults brought him to this. The abiding hatred. The absorbing malice. What has he to hold against me. My imagined station and its privileges. But why hate me so passionately. Me he was after. I am sure of that. What have I ever done. To him. Drawn breath. That enough to set him off. The mere existence. He's no disinterested judge of my sins. Our differences. A peaceful coexistence was all I asked. The social artifices which possess him. Like a rabid dog. Stricken with that, consumed with that. All but foaming at the mouth. His leer: But you wouldn't know about such things, being rich. What things. *Nihil humani.* Pain fear disappointment solitude abandonment lust incontinence yes even envy covetousness. Who have everything. What don't I know. Alike as two peas in a pod. Yes. I would have borne it. Bore it so long already. But now. No. The monster reveals himself. Man in form only. He's the one not to know such things. Kindness tolerance patience restraint grace. A case of form diverging from function. No longer now. He doesn't know how much alike. I've done worse than this. So human an act could not be foreign to me. Should have called him sooner. That's the only thing. A certain stability. The tension of opposites. Another level of existence. New laws prevail. Come not even to feel the strain. The strain a part of living at that level. A euphoria. But the equilibrium cannot endure. Only briefly can the organism raise itself to that level. Then something snaps. Too late for this. I've fallen free. Free. What will she do. Needn't worry about that. Land on her feet like a cat. Women do. No pole to grasp. The gift for it. Men go to their destruction, holding fast to the pole, imposing that artifice on the universe. Order. Morality. Women have no need for that assertion, that fatuous manipulation. They are the world. World within the world. The womb and all that dwell therein. Do well enough without us, God and man and the mediator between the two, known and unknown, palpable and ethereal, real and ideal. The peneal gland. No need. No need. It is like it is. It goes like it goes. As immodest and unapologetic as the world itself. How long have I borne this with me. Seventeen, eighteen years. That shame. And she no shame. No remorse. The way things are, the way they were. The Littlejohns' party. Why think of it now. Over. Why go into it. Children then. Forgiven everything. But then she said. What. The thing I hate about these parties is that you're the only man here worth sleeping with. An observation. Or invitation. It seems so long. Long enough for her not to remember. She was so young anyway. Young enough not to be held to account. Seven or eight. And I thirteen. Unlucky. Not the normal childhood. How did it happen. To think. Rain so that we couldn't go outside and play. The stillness, coolness of the house when it rained. The thick fermenting, woodsy smell. The vague gray light. Another world. Playing house. How. I touched her. How. She had the softest little lips when she was seven. The smoothest little body as yet unformed. The sweetest labia. My God. How. Playing doctor with the children of the neighborhood. Perverse. Dispassionate. Her clinical interest. The gross structure, the simple mechanics. And all that pubescent fire, that green lingering phosphorescent unsatisfied fire in me. The humiliation that fire caused me. That glow I thought as obvious as an odor, the odor of estrus, a constant heat, the smell of longing, the terrible longing. The fantastic structures I built in class and then the inability to move when the bell rang for shame at the erection. They all seemed to know. Bunky's joke about the naked girls running through my mind because they daren't walk. Found out. I thought. Found out and condemned. The shame of that. And her curiosity for which she felt no need to apologize. The cat's. Why did my face screw up like that? Like what? Like this, she said and made a mockery of my longing. Or: Why is it sticky like this? Or: Why does it get so red? I don't know. I don't know. It just does. It just happened. I don't know. Once. Twice. No more than that. An aberration. But then, when I was seventeen and had the curse still on me and thought myself alone with myself, bigger and redder with age, bigger and redder still with my coaxing, my fantasies, my exploits with the reigning movie queens, the girl down the street whom I didn't even like, and she opened the door suddenly and caught me redhanded. Oh, she said, laughing, I didn't know you were busy. Laughing, then sobering up. Officious, taking care. Here. Let me do that for you. No. No, let me do it. I can do it better. And she could. And she could. Could. So much better. Here, let me. Let me do you. The expiring gasp. Don't be silly. I don't have one. How can you do me. Say, can I borrow one of your shirts. That's what I really wanted. The pragmatic. Everything in its place. We've thirty minutes before I have to catch my train. Time enough. Time enough. Do me. But hurry. Hurry up please. Problem to solve in a limited period of time. Hurry up please. A Chinese box. Bye-bye, love. One of your shirts to wear on a hayride. Did she know at all what she did. She knew knew knew. She had to know. The signs too vivid. Pulling that line of boys out by the roots. Extirpated from an imposed innocence. Get me out. Let me out. Those old selves left to dry in the sun like the skins of snakes which have molted. Me next. Do me next. Me. What have we to atone for. Children's games. Nothing serious.

Nothing important. And so few times. Twice. Thrice. No more than that. Wonder that having broken the barrier we didn't give ourselves to it completely. But no. Knew wrong when I saw it. Some horror left. Whatever the desire. Do me too. And her indifference perhaps. Plenty of other playmates where that one came from. That time home from law school. Afternoon. Mama somewhere else, wherever mothers are when you need them. The familiar ringing in the hallway: giggling, hers; groaning, his. Burst in, already angry. Pull him off, push him out, throw his clothes after him. Her anger loosens her tongue: You're just jealous, you just want to be doing what he was doing. Here. You want it or don't you. Throws her legs up. The purple waxy obscene voracious flower. Some exotic plant. Damp, as after a rain. It's good enough for you, huh. I know, know what you've done, and Mama does too and in her bed too. At least I'm in my own bed. I slapped her then. To get some sense into her and to prove to her that she was right. Slapped her. Have always done that. The two halves of an hourglass, spilling from one to the other. Man and monster. Slapped her. And she just laughed. The horror. She knew, knew, knew what I felt and the advantage that gave her not to admit anything, to confess the sin, to be dictated to by a congregation of Babylonians. A totally modern woman, capable of making her own decisions. If it feels good. And me, struggling in that web. The last best hope for mankind. Shamed. Burdened. Well then, let her have it. If she wants it so badly. Give it to her. The horror. What will it cost her. She might even enjoy it. A new experience. Wallowing like a pig. Dear God, no. The turnings of the mind, soured like vinegar left to stand alone. Tireless turning, scratching. A child at play in his own feces. A sparrow picking fastidiously for the undigested oats in the horse droppings on the street. Ask her. She might like it. The horror to consider that suggestion. I am no better than he. Think along the same lines. Substance beneath the variability of surfaces. Even to think such a thing. Consider it. He knew his man. Great discernment. The depraved man still a man. Her legs wrapped around his waist, her ankles locked so that he can't escape until she is satisfied. His scabrous back, his pimpled butt heaving. Her laughter, her encouragement to a better effort. His grunts, the strain of his effort. God, leave off. These images will drive me mad. No. I'm mad already. To think such things. Ha. I am mad already. So come images and steel me to my task. I will save us yet. Preserve the family honor. My poor mother, with all her pride, her dignity. The tenacity, the unmitigable belief of the convert. From bare existence, from depression, to unimagined wealth and standing. She guards it like a tigress. The dreadful irony that she should have such children. Where did things go wrong for her. Such a daughter. A son so desperate to maintain the illusion that he submits to the harassment of a common thief, a fiend, a lunatic, and contemplates his murder. No. Not that. That would not distress her. Some men were made for killing. But placing oneself in the position where it would become necessary. Oh Loren, how could you. She's so, well, she's so little one of us. She does not even know her. Oh Linda. Linda. What is to become of us and what we knew. Goddam him. It can endure this. Leave him to his doing and brass out the consequences. Admit it. Sure. We're lovers and I don't expect you to understand the beauty of the love we know. Brass it out and summon the world upon its knees to honor those who show contempt for their opinion. Take my place in that corrupted pantheon. Damn their eyes and do it my way. Blue ice. Kees ice. King Cohn. Conehead. That astonishing survival. Roach. Roych. He thrives. Plotting, gaining. Corrupt, corrupting. Gaining steadily. No apology, never looking back. Gagging, gaining. No man of any dignity would have a thing to do with him. No decent man. And yet. He thrives. And I. Thumb my nose at the rest. Expose my nose. Survive it. Thrive. Like him. With brass. Kiss my ass. Way of the world. Adapt themselves to anything. Make monsters of us all. World within the world. Best of all possible worlds. No. No. Mad. Go mad. I can. They will the abuse upon themselves. Sure, you can do it. A world without values craves the image of one so certain of himself that it will tolerate and even invite anything. The ever renewed license. The only requirement is that the next act must be even more outrageous. Dazzle us, O ye gods, or we won't think you gods. The next time out, Mailer must consummate the act and in fact kill his wife. Sure, you can do it too. The world waits to be told what to do and has demonstrated repeatedly its willingness, at the least invitation, to go to hell. Let them go again then. My mother's pride will get her through it. Not now. Not now that she has it. Nothing will take from her what she has gained. Just let them try. Goddam them. Let him publish and dare them to do anything about it. Let him try and I will turn the law on him like a firehose and flush him down the first sewer hole. Let them try. The bastards. The bloody-minded bastards. The maggots. But. This too. This above all. I want to see him squirm. No. I want to hear him scream. And no one to share the sop with me. I want my revenge. The whole thing for myself. A hanging judge. Jury, judge, and executioner. No need for anyone else. Who. Why. I alone will do. Well enough. A pleasure. A duty. A pleasure in the closet. The joy of defecation. Rid of my own waste. His just deserts. Justice served. Am I not an officer of the court. And is it not my duty therefore to see justice served. Ha. This method, your honor, merely served to save the court the cost of a long and expensive litigation, the conclusion of which was foregone. This man is evil incarnate. A blight upon the face of the earth. A son even a mother couldn't love. I have seen my duty. I have done it. I see your point, my son. Go and be blessed. You have done well. Thank you, your honor. My lord, My God.


Bamberger and his cows. Or are they Wilson's cows. A time to think of this. What. Where. Where am I.

How. Home. How did I get here. Where is that goddam car. What time is it. Almost six. My God. How did I get here. Where did the time go. Where have I been. The car. I left the damn car. O God. Just kept walking. Rat in a maze. Innate map. Turn right here, left there. Do it blindfolded. *Voilà.* How. Nothing to do about it. But how. This terrifying surrender. Get along without the mind at all. Eat. Sleep. Turn here. Turn there. Maximize one's gains. Minimize one's losses. Habits. Undetected motives. Unconscious processes. Multiplicity of selves, in struggle for control. The voices. Voices. Gods and ancestors. Illustrious men. What great criminal still speaks through me. No. No time. Put time behind me now. Put Stanley out of time. Tell Ernest. No. Too many questions. Call a cab. Ernest always makes sure to know everything. He's perfect for the family. A family with things to hide. A conscience. Without ever asking anything outright, he comes to know everything. I wonder. What he knows. Susan. Or me. Not a mark on her. No little pustules to give vent to the corruption. Does she know. Not a sin unless you know it. Ignorance of the law is no defense. A lovely young woman, for all to see. Slim, still bronze from the summer sun, supple. The most fearless nature I've ever met. Because, I suppose, she's never met anyone stronger than herself, no one who could challenge her or ignore her, no one she could not dispense with by the flick of a wrist, an ash knocked without ceremony from the end of her cigarette. She takes no pains to hide herself. Suns herself nude in the backyard. Ernest is no fool. But then he did marry Willie May. Can't know everything. Have to call a cab. Or walk back. How long. An hour and a half. Hour and a quarter. Where have I been. Have cab pick me up at the corner. Drop me downtown. Avoid suspicion. Too many people already suspect. Mrs. Portman. John. He was acting strange all day. I didn't know. I would have tried to stop him. Only there was that letter opener. It could have meant anything. No. Walk back. Now. No. Wait. Came for something. Remember. Gun. Of course. Gun. To scare him with. Can't shoot him. No pleasure in that. Something else. Hanging too good for him. We'll see. Something. Our pleasure. But the gun. In and out quickly. Call from a phone booth, the office later. Held up. Won't be home till later. Have Willie May save me some supper. In and out quickly. The door. A stone. A leaf. The forgotten faces. Grieve. Grieve for the lost, the forgotten.

"Loren? Is that you?"

Oh goddam.

Coming into the foyer. Her face in careful disarray. Puzzled, expectant. Book in hand. The odor of lavender: she begins to smell like an old woman, older than she is.

"There you are. I thought that must be you. But I didn't hear you drive up. My ears must be going bad in my old age."

Leave it: she has explained it well enough herself. Pass on to something else, anything: a perfunctory filial kiss. "How was the meeting?"

She fairly glows with satisfaction, with her small triumph. "Just marvelously well. We are pretty much assured of the governor's support. That young man tried to keep from saying anything he could, but I think we got enough out of him and on tape to make it very difficult for the governor to deny us now."

Surprise. "On tape?"

She speaks with glee. "Oh it was Helen's idea really. I don't think we'll need it, do you? But it's good to have even so."

Old Max and his philosophy of government: the high reward for his condescending to do it: you have to get something for your trouble. Mildly, "I'm surprised Max agreed to be taped."

"Oh he didn't know."

Then he hasn't changed: the same arrogance, the same conviction that no one is as smart as he and no one therefore can put anything over on him. Serves him right. I say: "Well, I'm glad to hear that someone might find a use for Max yet. You'll be the first if you do manage to get any work out of him."

She smiles complacently. "Oh he's not so useful as a crowbar. But he'll do for what we have in mind. I know you don't think this a particularly big deal. But in our dotage you know you have to humor us old ladies. We have to do something to keep out of mischief."

Play along to please her; smile to reflect her smile. "You already do more than any other ten women in town, more than enough to keep you out of mischief."

"Oh but I must think of Helen too."

"Helen's old enough to take care of herself."

A certain resignation, but without sincerity, enters her voice. "I know that. But she is so little good at it."

We exhaust the topic in the familiar ways. "Helen's good enough at anything when she chooses to be."

But that takes her mind from her project. "Say, are you all right? You look sort of pale, out of sorts, something."

Surprise: that obvious. Another witness. Must stop her, say something. "As a matter of fact, I do want something. I just stopped by to get it. Then I'll be going out again."

Disappointment darkens her voice. "Oh Loren. I had so looked forward to having supper with you."

"I'm sorry, Mama, but I really can't. Just tell Willie May to put something aside for me. I'll eat it later."

Her eyes begin to narrow. "I think you must be working too hard."

I defend, "No harder than anyone else."

Her neck stiffens. "There is something the matter. I can feel it. Come here and let me feel your forehead."

Relent: it will settle her. Present my forehead: John the Baptist on a silver platter.

"Why, you're as cold as ice, Loren. You must be coming down with something."

Hasten to reassure her. "Mama, I'm fine, really. It's getting chilly out. That's all. It's that simple."

Her eyes dubious still, behind lids half-closed; her voice gains its authority. "There's so much you don't tell me, Loren."

I defend, "There's little I tell anyone."

She mounts the argument which she has always thought compelling. "But I'm your mother."

Change the subject gently. The depthless vortex. "Listen, why don't you have supper with Susan, and we'll have a brandy when I return."

Unmollified. "I can't. She's gone to the club for dinner with Max Bunting. I didn't know she knew him."

Chill rushes through me. Must stop. Can't. Must stop. Can't. "She's what?"

The blast startles her. She jerks her head back, regards me with hurt incomprehension, the look of the unjustly accused, which alters gradually to incipient indignation. Her lips tighten. "Why? What's the matter? You heard me, I believe. I made myself perfectly clear."

Laugh it off: raw bitter sound. "She's a bit indiscriminating in her choice of dinner companions, that's all."

Her pride rising to the occasion. "I think you're making a bit too much out of all this. He seemed like a perfectly pleasant young man to me. Nothing of quality to speak of but certainly presentable. And frankly I don't see what you have so against him."

My voice begins to fail me: not my own. "I have against him only what I have against any roué. A liar, a sycophant, an inveterate debauchee. A man without p-p-principle except his own salvation. A violator of the p-p-public trust."

She snorts, "He didn't seem that way to me."

The wild high wind. "What the hell do you know about it?"

"Loren, I am your mother."

"What the hell does that have to do with Max Bunting?"

A cold, cold voice. "Nothing at all, I hope. But I do expect to be spoken to in a civil voice by my own son. Your sister doesn't speak to me like that."

"My sister hasn't the reason to."

She allows the pause to gather ominously. "Do, pray, tell me what you mean by that comment."

Will not, cannot, cannot get into this. "I mean nothing by it."

She consents to let it pass; renders her word to the wise. "You could be more like your sister."

I will not bear it: cannot. "You mean I am to suck ass with the state's reigning coke king."

Shocked, sternly. "Loren."

I play with her, my fiendish play: "Don't tell me this has escaped you. His hobby. His little moonlighting at the taxpayers' expense."

Unwavering, bearing up. "I don't believe you."

"B-b-believe what you wish."

She cracks. "This distresses me, Loren. You don't think Susan knows?"

Her voice, her hopeful voice, clutching at its illusions, which I will crush. "Susan may be indiscriminating, she may be a fool, but she's not an idiot. She knows."

"I don't. I can't believe it. She's such a lovely affectionate girl. You could be so affectionate."

Stop: the irrelevant in anger, despair. "She's not a girl. She's twenty-five years old. And I am not the subject now. She is. Or rather her habit is. Her addiction."

Her voice crackles with righteous anger. How could I love her, not love her? The stilted imperious phrases. "I forbid you to talk about your sister in that manner. This is too much. Too much."

But I will not relent. "As you wish. But then we shall not talk about her at all. It's the only manner I know."

Her commanding voice, but with a note of desperation: "We must talk about it. We must talk about everything."

Cannot, will not. "We'll talk later if that's what you wish. Right now, I must go."

The pride, the will of a Roman matron. "We must talk now. This can't wait."

"I'm afraid it will have to. Tho even then I'm not exactly sure what you want us to do, what conclusion you want us to reach."

Sighs, for the first time cannot face me. "Loren, this is not like you."

A contemptuous laugh. "This is me, Mama."

But she seems not to hear, lost in her reverie, her anticipation. "I worry about you. So cold and distant. I worry about us. Your father. Your father's death."

Cannot bear that now: never. "My father's been dead for fourteen years."

She pleads, "Loren, be gentle with me. Your sister. We love you. You are our pride."

That priceless substance, ambergris: my extinction. But pity moves me: "I love you too, Mama."

"And Susan?"

Relenting, compromising: "Yes. Susan too."

Tears gather, begin to fall. "We must, Loren; must love each other. What's to become of us otherwise? I've tried so hard."

Comfort her, soothe her. "Nothing's to become of us. We will be as we have been."

Even in her distress, she detects the irony: a wild uncertain look, the like of which I have never seen before. "As we have been? What have we been?"

"I mean things will be all right for us. I mean, if they can't be all right for us, for people like us, then they won't be all right at all. Will they?"

Tears. How long has it been since I saw my mother weep. "But it's all so fragile, so ephemeral. Your father. Does our having money mean we can't feel pain or fear or uncertainty or disappointment? Your father." She chokes. "Was such a good man."

Cannot bear this: drives me to anger. "For God's sake, leave the poor man in his grave."

But she will have her way: find her way in the aftermath of the holocaust, find the broken doll, the shard, the table leg among the rubble. "But we've never talked about it."

Retort: "Some things are better left unsaid."

She nods vigorously her fine head, her face streaked with mascara; she sniffles for breath, comfort, love. "Yes. Yes. We should never have had this conversation. We've never talked to each other like this."

My mother. Love and hate. Pleasure and pain. The hand to brush the fever from my forehead, to scare the evil which possessed me from my cheek. Now that's enough of that, young man. I've never intended to kill a man before. Forgive me, I forgive you. I say, "I'm terribly sorry, Mama."

Even then she will not relent. "What is it, Loren? Please tell me."

Another witness but one I can rely on: Well Officer, if he did do it, I'm sure he must have had a good reason for it: the presumption of her own's innocence. Must go, must go now: *muss es sein.* "Nothing, Mama. I must go now. Tell Willie May."

"Loren."

I start, stumble, break free, call back, "I'll talk to you later."

"Loren. Please."

"I love you, Mama."

"Loren. Loren."

Sundown. The cold. The first sharp cold of autumn. Smell of cold: meat locker. Smell of burning leaves. One of the neighbor's. Mind's invention. Like the brain's opiates. Makes imagination easy. Pain and the release from pain as inmates of the same dilapidated mansion. At each other's throats. Undermining each other's projects. The utility of pain. Something not right here. Mind's mediation. Whether there is something. Objective correlative. Odell bending at the shoulder to his rake. Smoke. Where there's smoke there's fire. She knows. Something. Why had she to talk so much. Why had I. Collapse. Loss of all restraint. Something terribly wrong. Never killed a man before. How to make that up. What to do. Mama. So sorry. If I could teach the world to sing. Max. Coke king. Carrying on with an ash for a brain. Amazing adaptability. She will too. These artifices. A kind of catatonia: the twisted posture maintained forever if allowed. She will survive, adapt. Talk of the town. Embarrassment. Humiliation. Proof against them all. No question of her position. Only her just deserts. The perfect puritan. Outward manifestation of an inward grace. Turn inward upon ourselves, turn aside from the truth. What then. Turn to others for the truth. The blind, benighted, biased. The proud. The rude. The selfish. The self-important. Another's fall is my rise. Simple mechanics. What is honor. Honor in an age without honor. Tarnished prize. Comes to you with their fingerprints all over it. Their esteem. Play into their hands. Seek their approval. Matter of honor. Rat in a maze. Beast bred and trained to the moves he will make. No comfort in that. False comfort. Legal comfort. Temporary insanity. Couldn't help myself. The devil made me do it. Cold comfort indeed. Matter of honor. Tree falling in the forest. No one to know. The sound it makes. Honor. Esteem. Delude them all. Substitute their esteem for my own. Despise. Revile myself. The weakness. The mistakes. The failures. The falling short. You are not paid to make mistakes. Mortality. The chill. Try to shake it off. Early this year. Cold for this time of year. Untimely cold. Things out of season. Not the natural state of affairs. Death's season. Father. An old man napping in his chair. Married late, sired late. Died on time. For him. But for us. He and Kennedy the same year. Was that it. Students cheering when the news was announced. Laughing in the corridors. Fathers die all the time. The way it is. Families go on. Shift the ballast. Weather the temporary tempest. Go on. Blandly denying the list to port. All well. Nothing to fear. The hell, the hell you say. No worse. No worse of pain. The way life is. Pursuit of death. Go on, go on to death. These artifices. Structures built of matchsticks. Architecture of the secret instinct. Blown apart by the first yawn. Can nothing save us. Thought. Nothing from nothing. White on white. The artifices. Memory. Art. Religion. So on. Go on. Adapt. The mark of man. But to the unspeakable, the unthinkable. To that. Do anything one sets one's mind to. Reason not the need. Do anything one sets one's mind to. The great taboos. The supreme sociopathic gestures. Even these. Live with them. But at what cost. Go on. Strength. Resilience. At what point that becomes the mark of the insane. Obsession. Midas. On and on. With no notice taken of one's place in the world, in time and place. Time doesn't exist for the insane. Hold those postures forever. On and on. Oh were we to consider it, there would none of us consent to live. The final artifice. Forget. Suppress. We live, ransoming our souls for a few hours more and then, because that is not enough, for a few hours more in comfort. Better to die. If I could live so well as I could die. The horror. Is this all. Why can I not do more. The world, its beauty, its power, its indifference, mocks us in our ineptitude. Not one hour recall. Lost, all lost. No. Linda. She fades. No. Would not recognize her on the street. That part of the brain burns out. Memory. Now this. Recognition. Dying. Changing. Evolving. Devolving. Murder just a way of life. Nothing to fear. Do it. Do it everyday. It's better in the Bahamas. The old dispensations. That is it. I will have my way. Linda. No. Nothing to fear from the law. Make my own law. But secretly. Make it appear he did it to himself. How. Something will show itself. Artistic problem. Find the picture in the picture. Yes. I will kill the son of a bitch. Good-bye self. Linda. What choice. Rise above my own level. Prove myself a better man than most by my restraint. Accept responsibility. Acknowledge the love for what it is. I could. We could. Nothing to be ashamed of. But I despise that bloodless piety, that surrender. They have no right to it. Their mindless chatter at our expense, their gossip, their plumbless ignorance of our passion, their sniggering witness of our pain. Their imaginations take them no further than the image of one thigh thrown across another, the two vestigial patches woven together. Goddam them. They will not have this of me. Strike off restraint. A virtue made of necessity. Defy, defy them all. I will not be held in check. Linda. Teach the son of a bitch a lesson he won't forget. Ha. Macabre joke. No time for jokes. Yes. Laugh in the face of death. Little to choose between them. Find them both about the same. The living, the dead. An accident of time separates them. The walking dead. Not to think so much about it. Cleaving from fear to the repugnant. Whistling in the dark. About the same. So much for one's own life. But another's. Can one say that about another's. Wait. I did not do this to him. He did it to me. Violation of the tacit agreement. Social contract. Tolerance. Leave each other alone. He must be punished. But need I take such pleasure in it. What pleasure. I tremble. Cold. There is pleasure to be had. The satisfaction of power. The will to power. Libido. Death wish. Spectrum. Axes: time and instinct. Cycles. Seasons. Yin and yang. Yearn: the terrible unsatisfied yearning. Linda. Unto death. And burial. Urn. Dust to dust. Ashes to ashes. Thus it ends. The pretensions. The presumptions. So it goes. Gossamer. One's mind spinning a web to entrap oneself. The pride. The illusions. The mode of being. Spinning these illusions like silk threads. All for nothing. God. Is there nothing else. The good opinion of one's peers, of future generations. That will not ease one moment the pain of recognition. Awareness. God. Shall I die from shock. Dead now. Something's dead. Can smell it. A rodent crawled up into the attic and died. The stench perfuses the house. No escape. Death all around. Cold. Avenging angel. Terrible swift sword. Goddam I forgot the gun. No matter. Too late now. Other ways to kill a man, to make him kill himself. Fifty ways. Stick him in the back, Jack. Knock him on the head, Fred. Surprise. Scare him to death. Vasovagal reflex. Is he capable of feeling fear. Pain. Am I able willfully to inflict it. See him suffer. Certainly. Surely. Great constant. Nothing human. Murder. Always murder. Chilling sound. The *d* does it. Murder, murmur. The *m* softens, pleases. Om. But the *d*. Perfect word for the act. My God. What am I thinking. Run along. Bandy words. A man's life at stake. Two men's. And I measure the sound effects. My mind goes. Arrested collapse. Am I mad now, mad to consider it. Do it. Going mad. Continuous process. No distinct line of demarcation.

Each of us carries with us the seeds of his own madness. Am I. Flight of ideas. Rush of speech. Failure of attention. Am I. Silence. Silence. If I could teach the world to sing. That foolish song. Fills the mind. Nature abhors a vacuum. Clare Wilson. Bamberger and his cows. The Walker-Davis people pouring their waste into the stream. Upstream. Killing his cows. Homicide. Not nearly the effect. Bovicide. Bureaucratic. Colorless. Evokes no sentiment except in reaction. Fetal waste. But murder. A kind of onomatopoeia. Poetic act. Rhythms. Affirmation of self before nature takes its course. Birth. Death. Affirmations of the self require intercourse with another. Odd that. The hallucinations in solitude. Sensory deprivation. Conjured beings to keep one company. Even the onanist has his fantasies, his imagined partners. Do unto others. See ourselves as others see us. We are not alone because we cannot be. We are only to the extent we are not alone. And yet the essential paradox. Must die alone. Final affirmation. How terribly sad the pursuit of the eternal life. All must die sometime. That limit and the fear it inspires and the humility it enforces. And die alone. No one can reach me. Mama. John. Linda. They know but cannot reach me. Those depths. Alone. Nor me myself. The real me. New me. Those depths, then nothing. Infinity. The black hole into which I'm being drawn. The reversion. Stripped of his layers of civility. The shields. The clothes. The accidental appendages. The essential primordial beast. Sense of smell revivified. Know him by his smell. The long memory. Know what to do. That stage of our kind regained. When insult was a challenge to the death. Rutting season. A function. Incapable of love. No. He loves. Passionately. But the emptiness. Reach down and down into himself but still nothing. The farther down, the nothinger it becomes. Elusive substance. Is nothing certain. Only for this short time in this small space. Newton. Haeckel. The age of uncertainty. Anything goes. Nothing fixed and immutable. Then death. The last illusion. Fear death. The mind. Empties, fills. These fragments of meaning. Will not coalesce. Embodied nothing. Nothing. Nothing.

Where is he now. Oh yes. Turn here. Then to the end of the street. End of the road. Turn again. The steadfast tin soldier. New wine in old bottles. Enjoined. The blue light of the streetlamp makes it seem colder. Associations. À noir. *Golfe d'ombres.* How does it go. Mind like a sieve. Is nothing sacred. Will nothing last. Yes. Nothing itself. Joke. All else collapse. Maddeningly slow collapse. Yes. End of the street. No turning back now. End of the road. End of the tunnel. Light. Solution. Nothing comes from nothing. Nothing militating for nothing. Nothing ventured, nothing gained. Ultimate solution. Stanley. Poor slob. Has no idea what he has called down upon himself. Content to let things be. Their own. Course. Who is to say how they might have turned out. Can feel no sympathy. Can feel nothing. Numb. Cold. Make it easier at least. The initiation of terrorists is to kill a child. Difficult, the innocent. And so demonstrate to his fellows the assassin's commitment, willingness to do anything for the cause, and reinforce in his own mind his commitment by the horror of the act: If I have done this, I must believe passionately in the creed which called for me to do it. But Stanley. No more compunction than to flush the toilet. Anything goes. The age of incontinence. Abandon. All human principle. Dead. Dying. Elimination of the waste. The millennia have come down to this. Abomination. Outrage. Nothing to do about it. Precisely nothing. Call nothing to account. The poor dumb slob. Goddam him. Mind witness to its own disintegration. Dead. Dying. Toes. Extremities. Cold. Cold. It must be. Stop this trembling. Must. Stop.

# 5

No one of the more than dozen young men who had been privileged to fall in love with her, since the first rude adumbrated passion of Ralph Skinner, at age eleven, had ever managed fully to convince her that she was as pretty as she wanted and as each in his own way claimed. The ways of course bore striking resemblance to each, and after the first flush of pleasure at each new repetition she had reason to suspect that there was at work a conspiracy to blind her to the truth. For what reason the conspiracy had formed—whether it was malevolently to delude her and torment her with something she was not or in the hope of winning concessions she had not already made or whether they were weak and had to hunt in packs or whether they were fools and blind themselves—she could not guess. She knew only the curious tension of emotions she felt to hear the nasal, the guttural, the mumbled, the muttered, the passionately respired protestation that she was lovely. No, she wanted to say at those moments, raising her head from the shoulder on which it rested, I am not; but she did not and could not. To her dismay, she wanted terribly to be pretty—from that arose the tension between the hope that she had been magically transformed and the despair of knowing that, if anything, it was just the light, the poor light of a streetlamp, between the tenderness she felt for those who said these things to her and the anger and disgust that they should think they could get away with it so easily. She wanted to be what they described; and that she wasn't, or felt she wasn't, had been the source of a chronic mild disgruntlement which lasted through her adolescence. To her credit, she was too filled with animal spirits, was too eager to please and be pleased, was too caught up in the small adventures of life at that age to let the disgruntlement show. But it was there, the companion of her time alone, the face over her shoulder as she stood nude before the full-length mirror in the bedroom she shared with her sister and urged the smooth little body of her youth to develop.

Her disbelief was not the manifestation of a contumacious personality: tho freely given to her own opinions, she was not perverse nor so consistently irrational as to doubt the obvious. Rather, seeing nothing to gain by willfully sharing or concurring in the mumbled or whispered compliments, seeing much in fact to lose by doing so, she trusted her own eyes and trusted further that she was not deceived. More than she had yet experienced, more than the distorted mirror of a lover's face when she shyly laid herself open to him for the first time, was required to undermine that trust. She could see after all how inadequately she filled the mold, the celebrated Playboy bunnies, one of whose number was said to live, under a pseudonym, in Lexington, the mold which the boys themselves had designated as that from which would come the model of all young women, and over whose glossy images she and her friends had pored with the avidity of hopeful auditors. She could see how slow her little body was to mature and, worse, how far short of those just proportions it stopped. She could see—there was the rub. She could see that there was and would remain always something girlish, something promised but unfulfilled, about her—the short stature, the small high breasts, the trim waist, the delicate collarbones, the slender hips, the tapered ankles. She could see, and it mattered little that she never wanted for suitors nor that not a little of the attractiveness she bore for a certain kind of male was the illusion he could sustain, reviving the myth of Roger and Angelica, that he was to be the one to break her free from her maidenhead. She wanted it because she knew it was the one thing of those she prized that she did not have: she knew that she was good, she knew that she was smart; good enough, smart enough, as good and as smart as human beings could or needed to be; but she was not as pretty. It was her trial. But as she grew older, she learned to bear it with dignity and humor, tho not since childhood had she willingly consented to have her picture taken. Cameras seemed to know this about her and, as if insulted by her disregard for their abilities, disgorged always pictures of her which did less justice to her than she deserved.

Still, she was prettier by far than she was willing to admit. Her face was heart-shaped, with a little bow of a mouth over a sharply pointed little chin, with high wide cheekbones over slightly hollow cheeks, with a wide smooth forehead over large flashing green eyes. Her hair was blonde, a light blonde the color of honey made from clover, and, as if to spite her, curled naturally and, like herself, refused to be tamed for long, however vigorous the brushing given it and however many the pins employed to hold it down. Her nose was short, straight, and pointed but seemed, because of an extra allotment of flesh depending between her nostrils, to turn up perkily. Her teeth were very white but imperfectly aligned, again like her figure making her appear younger than she was. Her small ears were of a delicate shell-like beauty (tho only one man had ever noticed them and admitted the desire to place one of them against one of his own, to hear within it the vast unrolling history of her time, as one hears in a shell the shell's) and were, she had decided after much consideration, her best feature. Her skin was smooth and clear, not ruddy certainly, but neither as soft as velvet nor as fine and blue as porcelain: it was skin for a young woman of the world, a young woman of purpose, a skin capable of developing a subdural crust while retaining its smooth clear surface; and tho she might have wished it better, it had served her well and even now, at twenty-two, showed not the ghost of a line.

This evening, as she sat at her dressing table and waited for Loren to call, the face showed something only not worse than a line because it was temporary— the legacy of the outrage, a raw purple puffiness around her eyes. She had done this morning what she could with her makeup to hide her condition and she had almost succeeded. At least one of the men with whom she worked, apparently confusing a slight change in looks with an improvement in them and paradoxically emboldened by the change, had complimented her and then, after a slight pause, during which his tongue had crept along his upper lip, had asked her if she were free for lunch. Taken aback, in truth afraid that word of her lubricity had already begun to spread, she had hastily contrived another engagement and refused, then assented as graciously as the circumstances permitted when he concluded the interview with a slightly embarrassed exhalation, the words, Well, maybe next time, and a smart turning on his heel. She had hoped only that others' perceptions, tho unspoken, were as mistaken as that first one's had been—his murmured appraisal, how nice she looked— if they troubled themselves to notice anything at all. If only I can make it to the end of the day, she had thought, without having to explain anything, without having to explain too much; but she did not reveal to herself what comfort, solace, or resolution was to be found in the evening.

Her hopes, however, were shattered presently. At least one of the men, Timmy Brownell the art director, had caused her to start and recoil and blush, reflexive movements she had attempted to arrest, by asking her if there were something wrong or, rather, by telling her that something was and asking her if she wanted to talk about it. That was over lunch, as usual the chicken salad sandwiches they had carried over from the coffee shop across the street from the store, to be eaten as they sat on the risers which Timmy had installed, on which to mount the next show of fashions—See the Van Allen Collection, third floor—for the casual passerby and the window-shopper, from whose view they now were hidden by rose-colored paper completely covering the window and on which was inscribed, in bold blue letters, the plea to excuse their appearance while they prepared another display. Their talk until then had followed the familiar paths—the characters and personalities of their fellow workers, high and low, movies they had seen or wanted to see, plans for vacation still distant as the other side of time—but in listless and abstracted manner, at least on her part, a manner so different from the usual that it must eventually have provoked him to his unusual forthrightness and his question whether she wanted to talk about whatever was bothering her. She knew, even as she answered that there was nothing wrong, that she was only a little tired, that, if there were anything to be thankful for, it was that he had been the one to catch her out. Her secret, the fragment he surmised, was safe with him: he would not make free with it, run off to compare notes with their colleagues, conspire with them to put together out of their many views from their many angles the full story, a full story, as bad as they could make it, but not perhaps as bad as the truth. Still, his discovery had worried her. What he had discerned, another might, tho not so easily; what he had put together (or not, as he chose to do), another might, another who, with little reason, liked her less than Timmy did. That knowledge, however false, however imperfect, she could not allow to spread. But equally, she could not prevent it. The truth, some truth, would out. She would be known for something, if not for herself; she would be revealed, ridiculed, reviled. Already the wonder rose in her that they were right about her and she was wrong and not so good as she had always supposed. She was not mistaken in Timmy's loyalty to her, and he had schooled himself to discretion. But the very prospect of discovery added weight to the burden of Stanley's outrage and her complete ignorance of his intentions and made her, when she repaired to the ladies' room shortly after lunch and found herself alone for the first time that day, actually to groan.

She was a young woman, after all, along this dimension at least, of conventional aspiration. Of her moral acts she was the arbiter (with an occasional silent appeal to her Almighty); of her physical appearance she was the judge. But in the development of her career, because she felt as yet uncertain how to proceed to attain what she wanted, she sought constantly, by implicit measures, the advice of others. It was terribly important to her to be accepted by the people with whom she worked; and tho she wanted somehow to set the terms of that acceptance and to make them worth something, she also wanted very much to please. She would not please where she could not, would not beat her head against a wall, for she was aware of, proud of her achievement so far and would do nothing to vitiate it. But still she went far—allowing herself to be imposed upon by the more experienced, older clerks, cheerfully taking on new and unpleasant tasks, laughing at the wrong jokes, passing on the wrong gossip to the wrong person—if not exactly to curry favor, at least, by her lights, at that time, to prove herself one of the boys and worthy of their esteem. In her own estimation, she had started low and without the advantages other than those inherent in her; and then she had worked her way up. Her father had just barely a high school education, her mother less than that, while she two years before had claimed triumphantly an associate's degree from William C. Smith Junior College. Her father still labored and would always labor in the mill, her mother at the stove or, when times were bad, as they had been once or twice before, as a checkout clerk at Sears', while she had only recently been elevated to the post of assistant manager with the distinct impression left that shrewd eyes were on her and the implied promise that, if she proved herself, other, more responsible positions would be opened to her. Those were attainments to be coveted and she had given herself to the sacrifices they required with an enthusiasm all but equal to that she felt to surrender herself to those asked by her church. She had felt, with others, the consternation when it was learned that one of the great Atlanta stores was thinking of establishing a branch in Lexington and the relief when it was learned that those plans had been placed upon a high shelf out of the way and the common pride and satisfaction that they, Gordon's, were simply too strong on their own ground for one of the powerful chains to risk competition with them. Of her immediate friends, only Timmy made bold to suggest that perhaps the great store had counted the pickings too slim in Lexington in any case to assume the expense, tho he did express relief because, he said, whatever Noel Gordon's talents, one of them was not business.

The talk then of her trip to New York with the buyers (not to mention the private promise it implied of a bed at last worthy of their love, a larger setting, a wider world) proposed another stage in the development of her career and in her own, but she tried not to think about it lest she be disappointed should the talk prove empty. In that case, she was resolved, she would just work harder, with the tepid consolation to sustain her that some of her colleagues had never had the opportunity at all. These were not cruel or invidious comparisons, for she was not cruel; they were the evidence of her lingering uncertainty about her place in the world and how quickly she should rise in it: Should she be patient? Should she press her case more forcefully? She loved her parents and continued to live with them, sharing expenses, for love. But she wanted to do better than they, felt sincerely that a better life than theirs was

((( 165 )))

both possible for her to reach and, because of the efforts already expended, due her eventually. At times her ambition caused her a twinge of shame. They were good people after all, in the things which really mattered as good as any, and she had to fashion arguments to herself occasionally why the life they led was not the one she chose for herself. She had stopped part way and stayed at home, rather than struck off alone as she was able, she could tell herself; and that was a measure of the respect they deserved. Further, her achievements would shine honor on them. Her father would have another announcement from the newspaper—Gordon's promotes Linda Sims to manager—to carry around in his wallet and to show his friends—"Look here what Linda done"—but, more important, simply to have with him, a living piece of that authority to which he turned with a trust second only to that he had in the Bible. They had had so little honor in their lives: she could almost weep for the injustice of it. They deserved now whatever notice of their patient enduring presence they could get.

It was after reaching some such conclusion as this that, the third time she went out with Loren, she asked him to pick her up at home. She had never really understood the need to meet at the bus station anyway and her revolt against that arrangement had had its effect, a larger effect than she had intended, even that first night, when he had followed her cab home and admitted his defeat right there—to her embarrassment: she had pushed things too far—on her front lawn. Having made those arrangements, however, she had immediately begun to grow anxious, assailed by doubts and the intimations of all that could go wrong, so that when the event actually took place she could not enjoy the spectacle of Loren's courtliness nor her parents' pleasure at the court paid them, a court which emboldened her father to admit that he had known Loren's father, had met him many times, a good two dozen at least, when the old man, flanked by his managers, accountants, acolytes, like a prizefighter heading for the ring, made his way through the stupefying noise and haze of the mill, stopping often to greet new employees or to recall old ones, to take each by the hand, a benediction rather than the clasp of a comrade, and when, a good dozen more, each summer the company picnic was held behind the mill on a wide green meadow, a custom which the coming of the union, twelve years after the old man died, had ended. Loren had taken her father's revelations graciously. He had smiled that oddly twisted smile, murmured his appreciation when her father called his a great man. But already at that time she knew Loren's remarkable reticence about his family and silently berated her father for this unaccustomed, uncharacteristic garrulity and wished that she had not pressed this fine young man to whom she had taken so quickly into what she saw then to be her family's clutches. When at last she bore him off, when they were alone, she had had to apologize for their behavior. But he had seen no need for that and, to reassure her, had kissed her as one might a child with a skinned knee. Later that evening, he had kissed her in earnest, and she had felt herself stirring,

stirring to open to a man as she had never done before so that the next ten days, when he was out of town on business, were for her an agony of unfulfillment.

She soon repented of the shame she felt and, emboldened by his kind response, took to leaving him in their clutches for longer than he had casually bargained for. Her motive was not revenge. Her parents were flattered by his apparent attention, and that was enough for her. She felt also that something was due them, which they had been denied along the way, and here was a fair and proper knight to correct the world's injustices for them. But there was as well something in it, something small and insidious and unconscious, of the desire to get back at him for his failure to do the impossible, to introduce her to his own family. If one family were to serve for two, then it must serve the longer service. That failure could be practiced in two ways, overtly and covertly, and was. He might simply not take her to his home; he might also not take her where there was any likelihood of their meeting his mother's friends and having the necessity of introductions and, eventually, explanations thrust on him. They conspicuously avoided the country club, for example, which she badly wanted to see, and the two impostors of fine restaurants which adorned the town and even movie theatres. Their entertainment was found in drive-ins; their dining out was done at fish camps or truck stops or, more likely, at one of the four or five impostors of fine restaurants in the next town of any consequence, twenty-seven miles away, marginally more cosmopolitan than Lexington, and its rival in all things from who would attract the next corporation to build a plant within its bournes to whose football team (or in the case of the larger town, teams) was better. His house, all pillars and pediments, pristine white beyond the green lawn and the black ribbon of the driveway, she had discovered on her own from curiosity and never told him of her adventure. She wondered what his room was like and whether his athletic socks hung to dry in his bathroom as her stockings did in hers. She had asked him once about it, his room, the house, and he had said, mystifying her, that the best thing about it was the poem his mother, in her youthful enthusiasm at college, had copied out in needlepoint, some lines from Thomas Wolfe, to whom the region laid claim, and then hung, when she had the place for it, just inside the front door, like a mezuzah. She had doubted that that was all but had let the matter drop.

Their lovemaking, when it came to that, was carried on in his car. When their passion could no longer endure the constraints, because she would not go to a motel—"I'm not that kind of woman," she had said firmly—when the weather was too cold or inclement to permit them the coruscating dome of heaven for their shelter, he adopted the habit of returning to her home, after the rest of her family had retired, and breaking into her bedroom through the window she left unlatched. At first he had been dubious and had pressed again their only ready alternative, a motel: What if they hear us? But she had disarmed him with her candor, had caused him to smile secretly to himself and at the same time to draw closer to her, to feel confidently, deeply that he had not been mistaken: They won't. I used to do this all the time when I was in high school. The mill's already made Daddy a little deaf and Mama's made herself deaf too to be like him. The possibility of discovery then had been on at least one of their minds, but not discovery by that one most likely to do it. It was as if Loren had salved his conscience, the conscience which told him constantly to beware, by looking to his lesser antagonist and then given up the watch and therefore permitted their true nemesis to catch them off their guard. At the same time it was difficult to believe that Stanley hadn't even the dregs of decency to redeem him, that this heart was void altogether, so that nothing remained to move him of the first rule of human society, simply to respect others' claims on their own lives. They themselves in a sense had lived up to that rule: they had given him the opportunity, even if unwittingly, implicitly, which he might then abjure, to trample underfoot their garden of delight. And, damn him, he had taken it. He had gone mischievously about and knocked the heads off all the flowers. When that had not been enough, he had pulled the plants out by the roots. When that had not been enough, he had sown the ground with salt. The question remained, however, what he would do next.

Of that Linda feared even more to think. Foreboding constricted her heart, lungs, viscera, causing them to labor uncommonly. She could not force her lungs to take the deep breaths she drew; she almost panted; her great little heart beat rapidly. Nor would she say precisely what she feared. But in part that itself was enough, her silence, the unknowing, the doom still unrevealed. There was a certain peril, she knew, that the pictures might fall or be dropped into the wrong hands. But when she considered it, she knew that that peril could not be great nor the effects of that peril, should it come to pass, severe. They had done nothing wrong, she tried to reason; nothing wrong at all. They loved each other. There was no harm to anyone else in that. Their love did not offend; it violated no natural law. At the same time she knew the vagaries of the public mind, what monstrous inconsistency it could live with, how happily it might rush to accuse them of moral turpitude because they had done the only decent thing and kept the love to themselves, not sharing it with anyone else, to be sure, but neither imposing it on anyone else; she knew better still the mind of her employers, always ill at ease about the image they projected, a sharper image of the ones they sought to serve, and fearful always that those ones would desert them. She might be judged guilty for her virtues—the love itself, their discretion—that was the rub. The evidence now existed that disputed that. The love stood out as a carnal knowledge; the discretion, a public exhibition at which they had connived. The pictures which she had not seen condemned them, condemned them to be stared and pointed and tittered at, to be presumed upon, to be—and this the worst, as she had feared that morning—proposed to, to be importuned with the suggestion that this man or that would do her better service than the one she had chosen.

She could not bear to think about it and could think of nothing else; and each new train of thought, which she hoped would lead her out of her misery, succeeded only in taking her further into the dark. The further she went, and the fewer signs she had to guide her, the more she lost herself, the more she found cause to blame herself. She knew, she knew enough—that was it. She knew that, if the outrage could not have been prevented, had she heard that her brother had committed it, some malevolent act denigrating everything human, an act specifically of this kind, she would not have been surprised. The bonds of kinship between them were sad artificial things which, it seemed, had begun to fray and unravel on first use and were patched and maintained at all for the benefit of her parents alone; and, but for her will to acquiescence, she would have hated him, genuinely, passionately detested him, much before this. Her earliest remembrance of him was of fright: the garter snake he had hidden in her bed, when he was thirteen and she four; his shrill contemptuous laugh when she screamed; the fearsome teary vengeful stare he fixed upon her while her father beat everything out of him but a sound and consciousness until the boy's mother could bear it no longer—the swish of the leather belt, the man's labored breathing, the curses under his breath, the slap of the leather on the boy's bare bottom, her own sharp words to her daughter who had made the punishment necessary—and intervened. It was the only time Linda had ever seen her father thoroughly angry. He was from experience a gentle and retiring man but with the marks on him—an anchor on one forearm, the name Mary, not his wife's name, on one shoulder, both indelibly tattooed, the short sharp scar at the corner of his mouth—of another life at another time in a far part of the world, about which he never talked. That anger had been the mark as well, the brief elusive notice of the man who had once been but who was not, nor would ever be again, a man she could have loved as much as she loved the father she knew, a wilder freer man before his work began to wear him down and left him that kind of passion to expend, flailing away beyond all measure, as he had once done every week, that kind of passion now about once every half-dozen years. The incident and its consequences had taught her more than they and especially the latter had taught her brother, however. She learned two lessons: to take care and not to tattle. He had learned only that his persecutions of his siblings could not be quite so flagrant. In fact those things which became known seemed little more than the normal teasing an older brother visits on his younger sisters. But there were those occasions when, because the malice gleamed so brightly in his eyes, she knew that he would sooner have killed her: she knew that when he clipped a lock from her ponytail, stealing up behind her while she studied, he meant to be slitting her throat and when he filled her bottle of mouthwash with urine he meant to be poisoning her. She was the cat he tormented, tying a tin can filled with stones to its tail, then, when that proved too little entertainment, three or four cherry bombs.

The persecutions were not carried on constantly, and from one to the next she had time to heal herself and forget. The periods were quite long in fact and grew longer as they grew older, and he too seemed to forget, so that the last, when it occurred, seemed not to have realized an historical and consistent plan but to have represented the spontaneous seizing of an unexpected opportunity. He was home on leave from the army this time, shortly before he committed the accident which kept him from serving in Vietnam. Afterward she could not be certain that, having grown used to his absence, she had not grown careless also and left the door to her bedroom slightly ajar. On the other hand, perhaps his basic training had included the skill of opening closed doors without a sound. She could not say, could say only that her eyes had strayed from the mournful reflection of her little nude body, aged about fourteen years, to encounter his, gleaming lasciviously through the widened crack, however made, between door and jamb. She had started back, screamed at him to leave her alone, groped sadly, unsuccessfully to cover her little breasts quivering with indignation and her pubic patch as fine and wispy as the beard of an ancient Chinaman. He had not entered the room but neither had he closed the door. The eyes had burned from the shadows as steadily as brass buttons on parade. And it had been left to her finally to unshield herself, run across the room, and slam the door in that leering face. Her heart had shriveled from fear, outrage, betrayal. The unnatural act had bewildered her. She had felt ashamed. She had felt, finally, her utter impotence to do anything about the trespass. She could not bring charges, either formally before a tribunal or informally before her mother and father, without risking their judging her guilty or demented— a girl obsessed with her growing sexuality, about which she was already so unsure that she didn't know that she was not what they would claim—and his further and more serious persecutions; she could not wreak her own vengeance without appearing to join the fray and to offer him the next move, the next escalation. She could do nothing. And she had never forgiven him for it, this more than anything he had ever done to her, for the act itself and for the certain knowledge of her limitations. But shortly thereafter he had chopped off his toes and made a martyr of himself in their parents' eyes and so placed himself beyond her reach.

As if this were not enough, what her brother would do and the consequences of his acts were not the only source of that fear which had set her atremble all day. They promised to be bad enough, certainly, but she hoped that as in the past she would find some way to handle them, act and consequences, to deflect the point (if to suffer the grasping of the shaft), to live with the pain until it passed. What compounded her difficulties and menaced fully to transform her fear, anger, and outrage into despair was the looks, the stated intentions, the hard and fast purpose, and now especially the silence of her lover. He had never lied to her: there was no need for lies between them. As far as she was concerned, the matter was that simple. He had said that he was going to kill her brother. Her mind was innocent; she had not yet the years when her denial of her experience, her optimism, her feeling that whatever ill occurred things in general were bound to improve, would denote pathology. Her innocence could still be constantly renewed, like Aphrodite's virginity. Her every impulse was to seek the light, so much that she was easy prey to the melodies of Madison Avenue, the vignettes which portrayed so vividly the reunion of separated loved ones, tho the issue at stake, whether the sale of Coke or housepaint, airline tickets or telephones, was always in doubt. She made her own choice of goods and services, according to her own needs and appraisals. But the small domestic scenes— the college boy stepping down from the bus, in rural America, coming home—wrapped around the image and the promise of those many things simply for sale, rarely failed to move her.

Conversely she shied from the dark. Tragedy depressed, rather than cleansed her, so much as she would be depressed. She would not watch television shows which dealt in death. The books Loren gave her which broached the subject she read with chagrin. It was too awesome for her to contemplate, too expansive, too continuous, too alien; and she would have as little to do with it as possible, as little as an age, whose fascination with it was second only to its fascination with sex, would allow. Without hypocrisy, tho by abstraction, she would have wept at her brother's funeral. There was that rare gift in her which saw good and beauty in everything, tho perhaps distorted or as yet unformed, which accorded always the benefit of the doubt, even when there was no doubt, no longer. She was stern in punishment, to be sure, but because she thought it beneficial: the wrong, the ill, the evil of the world could be made right: the question was only a choice of methods. What could not be changed, what could not be made right, was death. Death was final, death was the end of promise, any faint, guttering, all but extinguished promise, promise even where there was no promise, nothing apparently but ash. Stanley's death would end any hope for him and, because she was not solely altruistic and believed implicitly Donne's word, for some part or piece of herself. She would not look death in the face; she feared to see her own face there and knew that she would see her lover's.

The routines of the day, in which she usually took such pleasure—the customers, the exercise of her authority, coffee at the appointed hour, lunch with Timmy, and so on—had cost her immeasurably and drained resources she had not known she had; she had thought almost moment to moment that she was not going to make it. But she had. The store had closed; she had riffled her paperwork; she had absconded, holding herself together with the uncertain dignity of one unused to drink with a serious hangover. It was not until she reached home that she felt safe. But there, in the privacy of her room, hers alone now that her sister had married and moved out, that force driving her on—her commingled desires for respectability, for advancement in her career, for the admiration of her colleagues—dissipated and the others—her anger, frustration, despair, fear of death, love of Loren—pulling her in opposite directions, with the tension of wires holding up a circus tent, suspended her, awake, alert, and motionless. She sat and could do nothing, aware only of her anxiety and the suggestion that her salvation was out of her hands altogether, that someone else would have to do something, directly to her, to get her moving again. She did not know what would happen but knew something would. Something would happen and she could do nothing to prevent it. She could do nothing and so felt that she herself was nothing. The conviction taunted her, teased her: nothing. The word reverberated with the insistence of water dropping from a leaky faucet in the middle of the night. This is death, she thought. This must be death: this awareness, but the inability to do anything about anything; this nothing. Whatever was to happen was now to take place without taking account of her. Her life was in others' hands, at the improbable mercy of fantastic elements, like those of victims crouched in the cellar as a tornado bore down relentlessly upon all they had patiently built. She sat alone, her trembling lips clamped, her little fists clenched, her fluttering eyelids closed, her face red and wrinkled as a neonate's, howling at the indignity of birth, of unwanted life. The ringing of the telephone then at her elbow, tho it made her cry out in surprise, afforded her a measure of relief: it prodded her to life, released some of that enslaving tension. She snatched the receiver and spoke into it with breathless haste: "Loren?"

There was silence on the line, a deep lasting silence, broken only by a muted click repeated several times. She in turn repeated her greeting with greater urgency and then, having gained no response, appended to it, measuring the words: "Stanley? Is that you? Stanley?"

There was no answer nor, after the first muted rattle, any sound; the line was as soundless as the four walls of an unfurnished room: a silence cracked and spotted with rain but complete and incorruptible. And presently, invoking a silence of her own, in a painful whimper, she restored the receiver to its resting place. "Oh God. Don't do this to me."

By the great pressure of these events, their remorseless sequence, their irreversibility, she felt reduced to insignificance. The abilities she had gained and been so reasonably proud of, her abilities simply but in so many ways to get on with people, to serve them and to win their service, had cruelly been stripped from her. Only her mere physical presence remained to her at this moment: no past comforted, no bright future beckoned. She had only the experience of present pain, which, because it continued, threatened always to continue. In time—in what time, moments, hours, she could not say—the pain established a location and became specific: it too was concentrated and reduced; it seemed that coils had imperceptibly tightened around her chest until she thought that she would not be able to breathe. That awareness made her situation immediately easier. The sole purpose of her life became to get air into her lungs. She sat at her dressing table and devoted her mind to drawing deep breaths. She could feel her diaphragm distend with each inhalation but could measure no other effect. She felt no fresh charge of life. The small dark inward corners did not begin to glow. Her extremities did not begin to tingle with the charge. Her head did not expand like a balloon and fill with hallucinations. Her heart did not slow its mad rush forward in the manner of a lemming. But she kept on, taking in the air through her nose, raising and lowering her head, in exaggerated rhythm, to emphasize the seriousness of her task. After many minutes of the exercise she still could feel no relief; and thinking desperately that fresher air might help, she crossed quickly to the window and raised it and seated herself before it.

The October air was cold, felt cold against her limbs, her body; but it moved slowly, indolently, with the confidence of the very rich; and after the initial shiver she took pleasure in its embrace. The moon had not yet risen completely, but already the backyard over which she looked was frosted with an opaline light. As she continued her breathing, she grew fascinated by the soft light, as soft as mold or the nap on velvet, the magical effect it had, and in due course she bestirred herself to return to her dressing table and extinguish the lamp burning there and then again to place herself dejectedly before the window. The familiar objects in the yard stood out with greater definition from the surrounding darkness: the coiled garden hose, the two crosses and between them, preternaturally suspended, the canvas bag of clothespins, the set of swings, now badly rusted, which her father had erected many years before for her and her siblings and which they now kept in place for her sister's children when they should come of age, the bicycle of one of the neighbors' children, abandoned in its awkward collapse to gather dew, beyond them a section of concrete pipe four feet in diameter left behind when the construction company two years before had laid a new water line along the edge of their property and now converted by the children into a plaything. Beyond the concrete pipe rose up the dark wood where she had roamed as a child and where her first boyfriends had taken her, or she them, in the recrudescence of some pagan rite. Beyond the neck of woods stood the Methodist orphanage, surrounded by a cyclone fence on which was hung the notice to keep out. A Methodist herself, she had always felt a measure of pride, along with that pity for the inmates, for the good works with which she was thus associated. She had not let it rest with that, however. She had taken the accident of her residence seriously and for years, since the age of seven or eight, when she first became aware of what an orphan is, had arrogated to herself the responsibility somehow to watch over them. Still it was she whom the church sent forth at Christmas as emissary laden with boxes of second-hand clothes and discarded toys for those, as their minister insisted on calling them, by shame to extort a greater bounty, the less fortunate. She never failed to volunteer, and they, with a certain amusement at the good works she wrought, her earnestness, her energy (among the wags it had been passed when she came of age that, if she wanted a child that bad, any number of them would be happy to oblige her), never failed to let her. It had been at her insistence that the summer picnic was established, when the orphans might run free as other children, for the day at least, on unfamiliar ground. It was at her insistence, over the official reluctance, that a program of visitation, one orphan with one family one night a week, was still considered.

At this time, none of that mattered: not the orphanage nor her determination to give homes to as many of those children as she could when she had the home to give nor the poignant desire for children of her own. Her mind passed over each quickly, afraid to alight, to take full cognizance of them. Never had she felt so far from the realization of her projects. She had never imposed on Loren, had never tried to bind him to things which he did not himself support, had once in fact, to the contrary, boldly absolved him from the responsibilities they drew inevitably toward. But at the same time, she had never not thought, or perhaps just hoped, that somehow it would work out. She did not count on it exactly. But she could not discount it because she wanted it. She wanted badly to be his wife and almost subconsciously had gone about effecting it, making herself indispensable, making herself perfect in his eyes. And she had almost, she knew, she had almost succeeded. But now the dream, the golden dream, was in eclipse, collapse, disintegration, before even it had been finished, realized, and allowed its chance for success. The deep breathing had contributed little to ease her mind; the cold, after the first exhilaration, now amplified her fear and caused her to shake uncontrollably, tho for many minutes, again a time without limits, she was scarcely aware of it and sat, staring vacantly into the night. Finally her discomfort took possession of her and exhaling in short broken gasps she rose to lower the window. But at just the moment when she took her eyes from the scene before her, she thought she descried a movement within that circumscribed stillness. Her heart began to beat faster, faster still, and hastening aside she hid behind the chintz curtains of the window and from behind them peered intently out. Nothing moved. The indistinct objects were as they had been: untouched, unmoved, unmoving, with the moonlight on them, growing like a mold. And yet she was certain that she had not been mistaken, more certain than she had ever been of anything that night, except her pain and that she wanted this time to pass, more certain than that she loved Loren, which she simply had not questioned, altho this was the single issue which held the frightful edifice of pain erect. Something had moved. She knew it. Quickly she scanned the yard again and then again, and then more slowly, forcing her eyes to linger over every object and identify its every facet, every part. She began with that closest to the house and moved outward until the stand of dark trees forty yards away blocked her view. Nothing moved. Nothing had insinuated itself into the soft frosted yard. And yet she was certain; her heart pounded out its rhythm of fear to prove it.

She had no evidence then to support her accusation that the sentinel, watching, waiting, was Stanley. But nonetheless she knew that he was there. She could point to nothing really, and every time she raised her finger the image she wished to call attention to faded before she could get her exclamation out—There he is! And yet she was certain, with the certainty which springs from necessity. He had to be there, watching her, whatever new fear it suscitated, whatever his motives, for then she would know that he still managed to avoid the fate Loren held in store for him. That last heroic gesture, to force herself under that lubricious gaze, that gaze which lay upon her like a wet blanket on a cold morning, was made of course to save Loren. So long as Stanley lived, Loren was still innocent, at least in the eyes of the law. So long as she held Stanley in view, she thought, no harm could come to him. It cost her dearly, to sit and watch him and know that he watched her. No matter how often she saw it, she could not accustom herself to that mirthless smile. They haunted her, that smile and the nasal laugh to which it gave way like putrefaction giving off a fetid odor, had haunted her for years, since that time when Stanley came of age to be entrusted with the care of his sisters while their parents enjoyed an infrequent evening out, since that time when he had awakened her with a flashlight held to illuminate his face from below his chin, that red mask in place, and frightened her so badly that from that time she was certain she carried forward the recurring nightmare of a cowled figure chaining her to the sweating cold wall of a dungeon and the childish fear of sleeping without a light nearby.

Nothing moved. But under the strain she succeeded finally in drawing an image from the silhouettes of the trees, a paler spot, which she could not otherwise identify, roughly the size of a man seen at a distance. She affixed her gaze to the spot and tried to keep from blinking for fear that the normal action of her eyelids would efface the indistinct figure. Indeed it did when finally her lids closed, and she took several fretful moments to recover the object of her watch. Even when she did, however, the image would elude her, tease her, pause to hover just beyond her apprehension, present but somehow unaccountable. It never hid itself for long, it never reduced her to despair. But it maddened her by its ephemerality, its fading in and fading out of its protective cover, the spare flickering indistinct figure in the wood. And in time, she began spontaneously to save her mind, a reflexive unacknowledged action, which turned her eventually to propose joyfully that she had made a mistake and that the figure was Loren waiting, as he had done so many times, until he thought it safe to cross the open ground and to scratch upon her screen his little message of love, to announce himself, a sound as delicate, prized, discreet as the scent of roses. How she longed for that sound those nights when she knew he would not come. How she longed for it now, the familiar gesture among the ruins which gives one hope that he and those he loves will survive and still love, the strand of song evoking an old time and place when things were better and promising by its playing at that moment of anxiety a better life to come. She felt terribly aged by these twenty hours; she felt that time had at last caught up with her. These months, these few, had been by far the happiest of her life, and in happiness she had not marked their passing. It was as if time had stopped for them and now that it had overtaken them and prostrated them in a rush. She had thought that their future life might just go on and on as it had, infinitely on and on until her need for children of her own became too strong, on and on. They had talked in passing, in the abstract; but so happy then they had not sought any change. But now the necessity for change, for something different was thrust upon them. Perhaps they could just run away, she thought, start a new life elsewhere, turn over a new leaf, where no one knew them. They were so happy, and her career and his good name seemed petty considerations beside that joy. No term had been set for their happiness; there was no reason why it could not endure, none but those they made themselves. They would have to make changes, yes, the necessary adaptations to altered circumstances. But to keep something so fine as this they could do that. They could do anything and it would be worth it.

Yes. She had never felt previously the triumph she felt to be taken in his arms. The victories of her youth, however satisfying at the time, were gains, she had come to see, of little significance to the world at large. No one now recalled that in high school she had borne the state's colors for the Military Marching Band of Red, perennial runner-up in the state's high school band competition, nor that she had been elevated by the good opinion of her peers to the vice-presidency of the Distributive Education Club during her senior year. Her volunteer work for the church had elicited the standard set of jokes about her piety on Sundays and her good sense the rest of the week. Her degree, for which she had worked hard, was, to those with whom she aspired to work now, only the bare minimum in certification they could expect (the better thereby to shuffle off the responsibility for judging her on her merits) if they were to invest her with any real authority. The other men she had collected seemed like so many shells washed up upon a beach, some broken by the storm, some whole and lovely in their wholeness but very small, and all available to the first woman who passed that way with interest and energy enough to stoop and pick them up. She would not demean these things because they were real, they were her own, and because she would not demean anything done at the honest urging of one's heart. But the spell they cast now was remembrance. She found it pleasant to take out occasionally the talisman associated with some almost forgotten act—the pin she wore denoting her office; the bottle of perfume, now long empty, the first gift a boy had given her—and by its agency to summon up the past. But at the same time she felt irretrievably separated from that past, not only from the past itself, moreover, but also from the present and the future which that past predicted. The revolution had taken place within her. The world was not the place it was.

What she now thought to be true of each of these triumphs of her youth was that each had been won in a very small arena; what sweetened the savor of her affair was the fact of Loren's experience. He was strong, as strong as wire, strong enough to run with her piggyback, laughing and screaming to be let down, across the parking lot of a truck stop out on the interstate, her his handicap as the man they raced against had his, a belly almost the size of her and a few too many beers, on a bet of ten dollars with an old football rival from one of the county high schools ("And I can still beat you." "Oh yeah, well, here's ten dollars says I can pick up that girl there on my back and still beat you to the other side of the parking lot." "Oh yeah, well, here's ten says you can't."), as strong as that tho even she could see, or especially she, that he was shorter than the standard male of his race. He was generous, or, as she called it, he was kind. He treated her with a finer respect than she had ever known from a man, a simple penetrating attention to what she said and a response in her own terms tho in a pattern of terms she would not have tried, the suggestion, for example, that she taste and appraise the wine they ordered with their meals, a ritual she took seriously, so seriously that she had once rejected with his approval a zinfandel, unarmigerous *mais parfaitement buvable*. Those were enough for any woman, she told herself; but then there was so much more. He just knew so much, had seen so much, had done, well, just about everything. He had traveled; he knew well places of delight and fascination, places which she could not find on the map, with names like Cesme and Budapest and Barcelona. The music he played was strange to her ear and other-worldly. He suggested books for her to read by men with names she could not pronounce and whose ideas, those she was certain that she grasped, troubled her. That Jimmy Carter was from Georgia did not endear the President to him (he asked, "How could anyone love a man of his station who insisted that he be called Jimmy? How could any President expect approval after that interview in *Playboy*? These speak volumes about the man's contempt for himself and for us."); that the Arabs had raised the price of oil (he asserted that it was their oil after all to be done with as they pleased) and created crisis in America (he denied the crisis on the grounds that so many people continued to drive so much) did not make them his enemies. He did not dance well but he enjoyed watching others dance; and several times they had driven as far as Columbia for the evening, to one of the discos near the university, in order to dance with an abandon denied them at home. She had asked him once why he liked dancing so much, all but implying by the question that he did it so poorly, and he had caused her an unexpected frisson of pleasure by saying that the mark of a civilized man is that he lives surrounded by beautiful things—paintings, books, music, works in bronze and faience and crystal, that sort of thing—but among which must be included, tho it is ephemeral, dance.

The pleasure had come of course because she thought that she must or might be one of the beautiful things he had gathered around him. He had never told her as much. The closest he had come was once at her bidding. Am I pretty? she had asked lightly, apparently making an airy nothing of her great defect; and he had answered, with a high casualness which reduced the problem in importance: pretty enough. She had never felt so flattered because she felt no shame to mitigate the pleasure. And even when she had persisted ("That's all? Pretty enough for what?") and invited his teasing ("For anything you want; for pushing people around the store"—she gasped, giggled, denied the charge—"for chasing ambulances"—she emitted a puzzled gasp—"for collecting dogs"—a louder gasp, a laugh, her leaping on his back to defend her honor—"I don't know pretty enough what for."), she remained pleased. His opinion in these matters she might just trust above her own. He had seen, she assumed, had known many women, tho he never talked of them. And of them, of all those he had had or could have, he had chosen her, at least for this time, for something. He could have, she had no doubt. He was a young man many types of women, from whores to homecoming queens, could love or at least desire. He possessed all the attributes; more important to her, tho a mystery of the universe even so, the deep apparently unconnected strands of herself responded to them like the strings of a violin to expert fingers. She had never felt so much a woman as when she was, each succeeding time, with him. She knew they shared this feeling. She knew he could have whom he wanted, but also, at the urging of every gesture, every expression, even every silence, that he wanted her. It made no difference to her how he wanted her. Her classification of herself among that set of inanimate objects, his possessions, did not disturb her at all. She did not think about it. Or if she did, it was to agree that, yes, in some ways she did belong to him because she had herself to give and had given herself freely to him. She saw nothing wrong in that: that was just the way the world had been set up, and one might just as well complain about it as complain that it rained every second or third year on July the Fourth and spoiled a good many picnics. She had things to regret—the secrecy he imposed, the access he denied her. But she knew enough of men to know that what she had with him was the real thing, and she had enough of faith to know that in time the veil they had dropped between themselves and the rest of the world might no longer be necessary. Until then, she would remain content that already she had more from a man, more of what she wanted a man to be, than she had ever had before. And if it should always prove necessary, if they and their love must always remain hid, well, she was just too happy to contemplate that now.

There had been times, many times, when she was certain they had all conspired to disappoint her; and she disappointed herself that, even so, she longed for them. One man only, she had always known, would satisfy her; but that one had been long in coming and the follower, if not the result, of so many unsuccessful trials, the last being the man she had agreed to marry, Ray Barnes, at that time the next in line to assume direction of a local lumber and building supplies business, but who almost eighteen months before had smashed his car in a drunken fury into a bridge abutment. That had been the pattern of her loves, to love unworthy men and to weep over the loss of them; and she had promised herself at the end of each affair, ever more serious, ever more demanding of her as she grew older, that she would not love again. She could no more not love, however, than a ball released can refuse to roll downhill. She had been made to love—by whose hand is not the question—and because she could not love halfheartedly, because she had a relative dearth of men and certainly of types of men to choose from, she had been made to be disappointed. The first of those, as usual, tho she would have denied it, despite her lucubrations, was her father. The pale green shoots of her childish sense of order and justice had been trampled on and bruised when, at age three or four, having burst gleefully into her parents' bedroom and espied her father naked, preparing to dress for work, his uncircumcised member hanging limp, she had brought upon herself the worst and the last spanking of her life. So much as she had apparently offended— apparently because, altho she knew she must have done something wrong, she did not know what—she also felt herself offended. And if it taught her, as so many other things thereafter, that she must take care, must pull the rein in on her natural exuberance, it also taught her respect for that exuberance, a secret love for that gift of hers, which so few shared and so many churlishly coveted, simply to delight in the things around them.

In another mental domain altogether, the punishment had roused her curiosity: rather than convince her of her naughtiness, the punishment had cast the precipitating fact in a peculiar and attractive light: that poor piece of flesh, by her childish reckoning, must be a thing of great value if even the mere sight of it made necessary so prompt and conscientious a retribution. It is far too facile a description of her life to say that hers was a quest like those of the knights of the Round Table, theirs for the Holy Grail, hers, let us say with similar symbolism, for a piece of the Cross, a panting perseverance, an obsession. Nor were her name and number written, in jest or earnest, on the walls of the boys' room at school. She was too genuinely liked (not so difficult) and respected (no mean achievement, on the other hand) for that and, further, had managed always to make her boyfriends feel that it was their faults they had broken up, to impose, that is, just that measure of guilt which would keep them quiet. But unlike the other girls and like the more daring of the boys, until she was old enough to persuade her doctor to prescribe oral contraceptives for her, she kept always in her purse a condom wrapped in foil, purchased surreptitiously for her by a friend who worked afternoons behind the counter at Brevard's Drugstore. The motto which supported this habit was also taken from the boys and revealed that pragmatism which later in her life would amaze and amuse Loren Owings: it pays to be prepared, she told herself with great conviction.

She had not been prepared for this, however, had not been prepared to scotch Stanley because, in love, in the arrogance of her love, when everything was meant to contribute to and participate in her happiness, she had tacitly willed herself into believing that he was not capable of committing such an abomination. Nor had she been prepared for Loren's threat, promise, intention to settle accounts, to raise in settling them, like a maddened gambler betting on a hand he had not even looked at. But, she thought, she was ready now. Somehow, given the opportunity, she knew that she could convince Loren that Stanley's act did not matter, that they could survive it, that they might still love and prosper. But she was oppressed by the dull throbbing ache answering the fear that the opportunity would not be given her. This most important thing would run its course without her, in contempt of her. No. She could not have that. The stakes were too high. She had to do something. Something. But there she foundered. So much was easily determined, but she had no idea how to bring her influence to bear. She could not ask advice of anyone. She could not call in the police. She had only herself to depend on. And with that recognition formed resolve, like an icicle in cold weather. He was waiting for her. He had to be. She would go to him across the yard soft with moonlight. Yes. The latch on the screen fairly leapt with her excitement when she pressed it with her fingers. She gathered a robe quickly around her. Yes. But then, upon the sill, she changed her mind. He kept watch for some reason of his own. He had his purposes which he would reveal when he came. She could not disturb him nor call attention to him now. No. She must be patient. She must wait as he waited. Their time would come. She must now wait as he waited. Besides, no ill could come to either while she kept watch. They had but to wait. That was it. They had committed no sin; they had nothing to atone for; they had only themselves to account to, and they loved each other well, how well they loved each other. They loved each other so well as to be one person, as she said. The terrible coils loosened then, as if her faith had been the key to them. They loosened and in loosening restored her. They could work things out, she knew; they could not help but work things out, so long as they had faith in each other. But in finding this release, she realized suddenly her fatigue. The tension abated, and despite herself she found that she could not hold her head up. Just for a moment, she told herself, laying her head on her forearm resting on the window sill; just for a moment.

At nine-fifty-seven, by the digital clock by her bed, the ring of the telephone called her from that state of near collapse, startled her, instantly resuscitated her fears. She knew her caller before even she reached the instrument, its dial glowing like a soft beacon in the dark room, on the little pine dressing table painted white to match the chest of drawers, the rocker, the beside table, which, with her clothes, a few records, a few books, the clock radio and the jewelry Loren had given her, made up her sole material worth. She knew and accused herself, but still she could not shake the drowsiness from her. It had insinuated itself around her and held her powerfully, like some dread submarine beast, below the surface. She moved slowly by her reckoning, held back from everything of importance to her, she knew, by her own weakness. It might already be too late, she thought desperately. Entire histories interposed between her and the instrument, between her and him. They were doomed, she thought with a desperate certainty; there was no hope. And yet she had to continue, she had to confirm what she knew already beyond any happy doubt. Her mind worked with an amazing speed, but like a wheel turning in sand, smoking, smelling of hot oil and burned rubber; and when she picked up the telephone, as if still half-asleep, she said, "Yes. No."

He was saying before even he had said anything else, or she heard him as if she overheard him in conversation with another: "Well, I can't talk right now. I just wanted to call, to see if you were all right."

His voice was a murmur from a distant world, a voice she recognized only to recall the voice she knew, the voice she called to now: "No. Please. Loren."

The husky voice demurred: "No, Linda. I can't."

She urged again, desperate to reveal her vision of things that could come before he rang off altogether, forever. "Loren. Listen to me. Please. I've got it figured out."

But he would not be stopped; he ran through her fingers like molten silver. "I can't now. I'll talk to you later, my dear love."

She began to weep. Her voice broke as she pleaded, "Loren, please. I love you. Can't you—"

His voice faded as an echo of hers. "Linda, please. There's nothing anyone can do."

She choked on her tears, heavy as beads of silver. "Loren—"

His promise, so faint that it might be denied or disbelieved, settled in her ear. "I'll call you later."

And that was it: the last inconsequential drops falling and dissolving: the moments of an impersonal time. Dead in one world, reborn to another: the plunge from that height upon which she had stood not twenty hours earlier as confident as a god; her last words were emitted like a moan and trailed her like the train of a comet, pieces of her falling away, never to be regained. "Loren. Please. I love you."

But now only silence answered her. Without purpose or intention, she returned the receiver to its cradle but then did not move. There was no place to go. Nor was there place where she sat. She lost all sense of herself, herself inhabiting space, acknowledging a span of time. The limits of her being dissolved, and she floated free, weightless, thoughtless, emotionless. If asked, she would not have been able to answer whether she sat still or fell through the ether. She had not the power over words to answer anything. She felt no longer any pain. No fatigue oppressed her, but neither was she alert. From habit she proceeded presently to disrobe, to recline. The clock beside her bed continued to blink the record of time's passing. The risen moon cast a brighter glow upon the yard and the image at the edge of the wood grew dimmer. She slept. In her hand she grasped, while she slept, a packet of papers tied with a ribbon, the poems Loren had written, some for publication under a psuedonym before she knew him, but some especially for her and not for publication.

In another part of the house, her father asked her mother where their daughter was and received the answer that she had said she had a hard day and was going straight to bed.

Later, a hobo, making his eternal pilgrimage along ways always familiar because always alike, saw a man he could not describe steal to the back window of a house he could not recall, pause there, then steal away again, a mystery insignificant in comparison with the thousands he had already seen and on which he did not waste a second thought.

At that moment Linda was in the throes of a nightmare. She tossed spasmodically, enshrouding herself in the sheet and blanket which covered her, and threw her arms up to protect her face. She dreamt that she had been incarcerated in an old stone abbey abandoned by its order. The clerestory windows had been filled with stone; the only light came from candles, one of which she took from its stand to light her way. The nave of the church was deserted. The only sound, she thought, was the whispering of the wind beyond the stone walls. Her white linen gown was sleeveless and her feet were bare, but her attention was solely on escape and she did not notice the cold. At last she found a door, oaken, thick and coarsely grained and furnished with a large loop handle of wrought iron. She began to pull the door open when a new sound reverberated through the building, a wail imploring her not to open the door. But since she assumed that that was the command of her captors, she pulled harder and drew the great door open. It had moved only a few inches when a force like the wind came suddenly to her aid and threw the door back, knocking her from her feet. The whisper she had heard became the rush of wings, in syncopation with the screeching of thousands of tiny tormented beings. She felt then as she reclined that she was witness to the fall of the damned, in which she had conspired but among whose number she herself belonged. She groaned with her betrayal. Then, when one of the warm furry little bodies fell into her lap and began to scratch instinctively at her breast, she screamed.

She sat up in bed, her eyes wide with horror, her mind grasping to arrange the depthless objects of the room. There was no sound in the house; the beating of her heart was loud and rapid in her ears and silenced the immemorial sounds of the night—the dripping faucet, the creaking floorboards, the baying hounds, the distant plangent whistle of a freight train. And yet she heard her duty urgently calling her; and not knowing quite why, hoping against hope, she extricated herself from the sheets she had wound about her and crept on tiptoes to the window. Carefully she drew back the curtain enough to see out. A new form had been set in the yard, a box of some sort, blank, anonymous, a monolith. It was some moments before she became aware that the object was not in the yard but was affixed to the screen, was not a box but a piece of paper.

As she scrambled gracelessly out of the window, careless of the cold and the dew and her nakedness, she thought it must be a note from Loren: perhaps he had not been able to rouse her, perhaps he had intended not to disturb her but only to leave this little testament of his love. Her first touch, however, revealed her mistake: the glossy paper could only be a photograph. She hastened inside, relatched the screen, lowered the window, let the curtains fall loose, then illuminated the lamp beside her bed. She knew the picture even before her vision had completely cleared, knew and accepted it because she could not refuse to accept it; but when presently she committed the photograph to flames, she did so as if stunned, as if in a trance. The picture was of Stanley: he lay prone, some fifteen feet from where the photographer stood; his arms described an unfinished circle around his head; his left knee was bent, his head turned abruptly to the side. The impression was of a man in repose. But around the figure was circumscribed a ring of fire.

## 6

So, this is what I have to say about what he done and what I done. And this is the way I have to say it, putting it down on tape, without the looks or pauses or interruptions of anyone else to direct my thoughts, but only the low steady hum of the machine winding and unwinding. Hopefully, I'll get it all down where it should be. Hopefully, I won't ever have to get it out again. There's just a lot I can't say right now, what will happen and what will become necessary. Time will tell like it does, and we will just have to wait for it, all of us, all of us except Stanley Sims.

I don't know now whether it's because I know him so well or because I scarcely know him at all that I could tell such a thing about him, just watching him walk up that hill toward me, could tell he done something he was tearing himself apart inside over, or whether it's because after a while at this job you sort of develop a sixth sense for this kind of thing, some few of us at least, or whether that sense is what makes you take the job in the first place. Of course anyone could tell something was the matter. I mean, even at that distance I could see he looked like one of the damned in hell, his shoulders stooped to the roll of the hill, his face hollowed out and ready to collapse. But there could be any number of other reasons, public and private, for that show and the fact that he came straight at me, slow and steady, would have thrown most other people off the track that he had something to do with this, something to hide, something to confess, something another man would have to confess. That's where what I know about him came into play. I knew he wasn't the kind to run or hide tho equally I knew he wasn't the kind to put his head on the block for you. I knew he was among the bravest men I had ever met, capable, like he done once, of going unarmed into the house of a fugitive, a black man holding his wife and children hostages against the world, and talking him out without a shot fired on either side and then standing up beside the man in court, the kind of man to face his own and others' troubles square, the kind of man you would want with you in a foxhole except for the fact that for as long as I've known him it's been impossible to separate the bravery from the foolhardiness. I mean, it seems like for as long as I've known him he's been taking bets no sane man would touch and accepting dares to do things no one else would do, like jumping off the trestle into the reservoir at night, when we were still back in high school, a leap that no one else had ever made by daylight. We thought it would kill him, and here he come up laughing and sputtering and damn if he didn't do it again, scramble up the bank and run out along the track and leap, leaving the rest of us to watch or, because it was too dark to see anything, to wait and listen and fidget and wonder why none of us were so brave. The next day we all went out again and one by one jumped off, and we were right—it nearly killed us. But there he had done it all before us, so we couldn't not to do it, and so we did it, one by one, and then came scrambling up, laughing with relief, to find him smiling and shaking his head and saying that we were the fools, that if he had seen how high that bridge was the night before he would never have gone off it. That's part of his way too. He don't mean to put anybody down. It's himself he's always testing, not anybody else, like he always had something to prove that no one else doubted or something to make up for. That's what I mean when I say I really don't know him that well at all. As good friends as we've been, as much as I've liked him, I've just never felt entirely comfortable with him—I simply never knew what he would do next. On the other hand I do know him well enough—his bravery or his recklessness, his pride, his store of anger, his sense of right and wrong—to be relatively certain he was capable of doing anything. He is different in that regard, maybe not any better, but different than the rest of us, different enough so that even those pretty much opposed to and envious of him held him pretty much in awe tho I suppose there's still pretty few who wouldn't think it justice for him to be brought low for a change, even if it was by his own hand.

So, you come being able to know such things or you get to know such things after a while at this job, and like in anything some know them better than others but there're none of us will question it, how you know which alley is safe and which you must go down with care, so long as it continues to work, to keep you alive. You just know it, who to trust and when, when to duck, what to look for. And him I've known for, I guess, fifteen years, and you could say that that's it, and maybe there's something to that too after all. I mean, it's just natural to suppose that if you know someone that long you actually know him. But Loren is the exception. There's nothing natural or ordinary about him. Somehow the ordinary rules by which you judge other people don't apply in his case. And no matter how close you get to him, or how close you think you should be to him after what you'd done together, you soon realize that he's still a long way off and that you're never going to close the distance on him. Tho I didn't know it at the time, I had my first lesson in that the first time we met. We were in junior high then and playing football against each other for the pipsqueak bragging rights in the town. And there he come squirting around end, and I slid over to try and get an angle on him, and damn if he didn't turn suddenly to face me, hesitate just a moment, then duck his head and try to run over me. I had just time enough to duck my own head before we collided. They tell me we both sat straight back down like the halves of a cracked nut. But all I can remember of it was a lot of lights going on and off and him sitting in the middle of them, smiling at me. That is kind of hard to take when you're trying to prove how tough you are and you already outweigh the other guy by twenty-five or thirty pounds. And it wasn't until the next year, when we entered high school and met in more conventional fashion, that I found out he played the rest of that game in a daze. But even in telling me that he managed to get one up on me. He was smiling that sort of crazy lopsided grin of his when we met, half smile and half something else, half sneer maybe, and the first thing he said to me was how that blow knocked him a rung or two lower on the IQ scale and placed in jeopardy his Harvard education, which his father promised him, and how he was thinking of suing me for loss of future earnings. Well, I tell you, I didn't know what to think. That stutter of his, that smile, were enough to make anyone think he really had been hurt, and I was already looking over my shoulder for the law when he said he supposed he didn't have much of a case for damages since he learned very well to run over little ones instead of big ones in the future, and he was afraid the judge would find him actually smarter than he was before, whatever the Harvard people had to say. After that we became friends tho I guess you could say that he's always been a better friend to me than I have to him. Maybe I've just always been a policeman at heart, willing and able to suspect anyone of anything, short-changed when it came to passing out the normal store of trust and kindness at birth. I don't know. But then I'm not the question.

So, there he was coming at me up the hill. And already I knew, in that few moments, that he done it, something, because I knew he could do it and get away with it, irregardless. The first of those is not so great an accomplishment. Only a few people aren't able to kill at all under any circumstances. A great many more than would like to admit it can be moved pretty easy to a certain kind of killing. They might hate themselves afterward or they might not. Like as not, they won't. But at that critical instant they make the choice they have to make. The difference between them and Loren is that they wouldn't know how to get away with it even if they knew it was the right thing. The difference between Loren and those who do it for sport or for a living is that he might not choose to get away with it. He wasn't likely to confess. That wasn't his way. Besides, if I was right, if he knew Stanley at all, he would know that he was worth little else than killing and that nothing was served by him losing himself over nothing. But he might have made it easy, for whatever reason of his own, for the truth to be found out. You just never knew with Loren, what he thought important and how he thought that important thing should be worked out. I don't know what he was working out and why when he sent me and my wife a lovely gift when we were married, a silver tea set which the poor girl nearly wept over when she opened it and now wears her arm out polishing, tho I neglected to invite him and hoped in my heart that he would never hear about it. And then the box arrived, a big box from Gordon's, and now it sits on the sideboard I rushed out and bought—the damn thing if we were going to keep it, and my wife would hear nothing of returning it, had to have a piece of furniture suitable to it—a ready reminder of my meanness. There are some things a man shouldn't ask, just as there are some he shouldn't be asked to do. I've never asked how much there was between them, when she first came to town to do her nursing at the General Hospital, before we met and fell in love. I know they went out a few times. Some day, when it don't matter, I might ask her, tho she's not the kind to tell me things I have no need nor right to know.

The church sits on a rise at the end of a mile of dirt road, which they tell me they are going to pave when the renovation is finished. That will be a long time now. I know enough of fires to know one that will loosen every nail in a place, and this was one of them. Even the fact that it was so far from any water didn't matter. That building was just made to burn, and the surprising thing was, I guess, that it hadn't given up the ghost before this. Even the fact that my men were on the scene that quick, quick enough to see at least that there was a body inside but not quick enough to get it out, didn't help. That was luck, of course. Or bad luck, if you were Donnie and Al and had to see what they then had to tell, the man staggering around like a punch-drunk fighter looking for his corner, before he fell for the count. It certainly was a relief to them to learn that it was Stanley they saw go down. They just happened to be driving by and saw the glow and went off to investigate, and there it was in flames. But it wasn't until they saw the body trying to find a way out that they knew they were going to have a night of it. The body was the thing that got me out too. Now no one likes to have his nights disturbed, but especially police officers. But there doesn't seem to be much help for it. The violent acts, the tragedies, come and go according to their own clocks and we have to go running out into the night to meet them. It takes its toll. And all the way out there I thought it must be some teenagers whose prank had got out of hand and I was going to have to visit some parents to give them the news or, in some ways worse, ask Donnie to do it for me. But by the time I got there, they had found the car and put a make on it and had the case wrapped. We've been after Stanley for a good while now, and my men were just about ready to go the short way around and make sure he did something they could catch him on. Then, suddenly, here he was, stopped cold by his own malice, whether he had in fact set the fire himself or merely fallen out with one of his accomplices and fallen prey to him. There he was; there was nothing to it. Donnie and Al were pleased as pigs in mud, the kind of pleasure doubled by the relief that the body was not some innocent bystander, tho they tried not to show any of it. But then I saw Loren, that stoop, that hollow stare, and I knew there was more to it than that.

He was dressed like he dressed in a hurry, with no notion of the season. He had buttoned his shirt wrong, leaving the collar open, and he wore no socks inside the thin loafers with the brass bar across the top he had on. His hands were stuck in the side pockets of his overcoat but it wasn't buttoned either and hung loose, open in front. His hair looked like it had been combed with his fingers while he drove out. He came right at me and stopped beside me and stood staring at the fire. The unsteady light made the hollows of his face deeper and more frightening, and I felt that I could easily be standing beside a real ghost on a real Halloween. Apparently he was going to leave it to me to speak first and in due course I obliged him: "Evening, Loren."

At that he didn't waste time coming to the point or maybe trying to find out what we knew. "Evening, Warren. Thanks for calling. Can you tell me what happened?"

Well, I decided I might as well start right in myself, so I said, "I was hoping you'd be able to tell me."

But right there he confirmed he was not going to help me out at all: "I think the county's paying you too much, Warren. Most grown men and a good many boys wouldn't need a second opinion that that's a fire."

I never learn; I've never been able to go back at him the way he comes at me, but I tried. "Well, there's always a job on the force for a smart young man to keep us from making mistakes like this, if you're interested."

He said, grimly, I thought, and without expression, "No, not me. But I'll keep my eyes open; and if I run across anyone like that who might be able to help you out, I'll send him along."

There wasn't much for me to do but to express my appreciation, and for some time we stood beside each other staring at the fire and not saying anything else. I had no idea what he was thinking; nothing gave his thoughts away. But my mind was whirring like a turbine, and I knew I had to say something or burn the thing up. I decided I had to press a few points and see what happened, like a doctor tapping and palpating and asking does this hurt. I started easy: "Your mother must be pretty upset."

The grim even tones answered me. "She will be, yes. She doesn't know yet. I took the call. Ever since my father's accident, she hasn't had a phone in her bedroom. I didn't want to wake her until I saw how much damage was done."

I made conversation. "What do you think she'll do now?"

He replied in kind. "I expect they'll try to build it back."

And so on, neither of us looking at anything but the fire and my mind beginning to smoke. "Well, that's good. We need something like this around here. Something to focus our pride on, if you know what I mean."

He objected, "No, I really don't know what you mean. I've never really understood the fascination with this project."

His tone had not changed; but before I could account for the divergence and despite myself, I made what I thought must be the standard defense but let it peter out in time to hear his murmured protests. "Ridiculous, ridiculous. This mania for the ugly or mundane, this conviction that because it is and is ours, it must be beautiful and worth saving."

As even as I could I said, "You infer you had a pretty low opinion of it."

But he had caught himself up short. "I've no practical opinion in the matter at all. It won't hurt. It wouldn't've hurt."

For the next several minutes I prodded and poked, slowly, without system, without doing too much damage nor gaining any significant knowledge. Sometimes we spoke, sometimes we just watched the fire, until finally I felt I had to make my move and then saw myself, when it was already too late, like a boy swapping yarns with a new acquaintance to impress him but doing all the giving and none of the receiving, neither of new stories nor of esteem. "There's something else you ought to know."

I paused for him to be curious. But he kept me waiting and never once took his eyes from the fire to face me. The light made a bronze mask of his face; his features did not move. He said at last, making it a statement rather than a question, "What's that."

I paid it out: "There was a man inside that building when it went up."

Imperceptibly his features seemed to have contracted to an incredible hardness; his voice was almost a whisper. "Oh, how do you know?"

I let him have it as deftly as I could. "Donnie saw him right after they got here."

At last I had a small reward for my trouble, the hint that my knowledge was true. He queried, he exclaimed in the same voice, a voice, I recall, not much above a whisper, tho charged with an incredible urgency: "Saw him!" But more even than that which let me know I'd made my point was that at last he turned to face me. His features kept their hard cast; the line of his jaw was still sharp, the set of his lips still firm. But his eyebrows had risen in two thick arcs, and his eyes seemed to stand out from his face, in surprise or fear or doubt, specific or unspecific. I thought then that that might do it, that simple little partial truth, from which he could take too much, and that he would crack. But I knew really that was too much to hope for. It was far more likely that he would never crack, never, and now he caught himself, said quietly, "You mean, the man who set it."

With as much carelessness as I could raise, I turned the screw another thread. "That's what we think. Donnie seems pretty certain of it. We know who he is."

I genuinely don't think I could have stood it; I nearly couldn't stand being the one to turn the screw. But he did, kept after it or me like I did after it or him. He whispered, "You've caught him then."

"Didn't have to," I said, turning from him to face the fire. "He was already caught for us. In there. Donnie and Al just couldn't get him out."

So I didn't really see what I thought I saw. With a sigh like the air rushing from a punctured tire, his head fell forward toward his chest. But he caught it almost as quickly as it started and so, except for the sound, I can't be sure. When I did look back at him, he was again under that incredible control, with his mind already after us. "Then how—? Wait. You had to identify him by something. His wallet or something."

I gave him most of it then, even saving him the trouble of having to lie, if that's what he had in mind. "Car's out back. We ran a make on it. You remember Stanley Sims at the high school? It's him."

He paused only a moment before answering, with an unconcealed distaste, "Yes, I know him."

His admission, I suppose it was, made me bold. "Any idea why he might do a thing like this?"

This time he was a long time answering, while we stood together and warmed ourselves and made our plots the mirror images of each other's. At last he spoke. "I'm full of ideas, Sheriff. I think you better ask his family."

I tried not to let him off the hook. "I plan to do that. But right now I'm checking with you."

So there we were and he made me see it, that he knew I knew but that he wasn't going to help me. "Why are you asking me, Sheriff?"

I made as little of it as I could but maybe gave too much away doing it. "You know how these things are.

You ask anyone, even those with no reason to know anything, in the hope they know more than they think."

He shrugged. "I'm afraid I'm not going to be much help to you."

I saw nothing to do but press on. "Don't even care to speculate a bit?"

He was quick to answer now. "Now I know we're paying you too much, speculating being what it is, if you've got to ask me to solve your problems for you."

I said, "I don't know that I have a problem, but say I just admire the quality of your mind."

He spoke softly, distantly, like some wise man in a cave, speaking on those things no longer of any concern to him. "Oh, you have a problem."

I decided this time to let him play me along. "That right? I don't seem to see it. There's no problem I can see with the way Donnie reads it."

He laughed then, a curt coarse laugh of no purpose, and said, "Well, you want something to chew on, Sheriff, chew on this. Sims was thought to be involved in all sorts of crimes around here, wasn't he. Burglaries, car thefts, drugs, even simple vandalism. In a small way of course, but not so small he constituted only a nuisance. In fact, if I infer correctly, just about anything you couldn't put your finger on, you added to the list of those you wanted him for. He wasn't big time, but he was enough to make you want to get rid of him. Now even a man that small has to have partners or associates of some kind, people to sell the stuff to, people to supply him. What if those others got wind of something, thought Sims was holding back or letting too much go, was making himself dispensable."

I interrupted. "If he'd been talking too much, we'd've heard it."

The effect was not the one I wanted. He fell quiet with the comment that he had no doubt of our abilities. And it was up to me to keep the theory growing. "You're saying he was murdered then?"

He answered disinterestedly, like he was suddenly bored with the game. "It's only a suggestion."

I tried to urge him on. "Got any others?"

But he'd decided that he'd had enough. "No."

And I had to find another line altogether. I tried the most direct one for want of another. "What did you think of Sims?"

He let several long moments pass before he spoke again and then he spoke so soft I couldn't be certain he did stutter as he used to, rippling over a letter or two like a stream over a hidden rock. "You don't make it any easier, do you?"

He spoke so soft in fact, almost like he was speaking to himself, a sort of commentary on the way things are, that I was not sure even that that was what he said; but it sounded like that, and I answered like it was. "No, I suppose I don't." Then added, "You knew him?"

That seemed to shake him up, to bring him back to reality, and I almost regretted my haste. His face had softened during the brief period, with something like sorrow or pity; but my urgency made those feelings, if that was what they were, disappear and his face grew hard and determined while he gave me Stanley's character. "Yes, I knew him. I've never met a man who so deserved to be without friends. He hadn't one quality you would want to teach your child, except perhaps tenacity, and did have a considerable number which should be crimes as well as sins, like cruelty. I hated him with a passion and a clear conscience both, in the flesh and in the abstract."

I tried to make something out of little. "You make it sound like he's already in his grave. You seem pretty certain it's him in there."

He answered, "It's him." Then added, so that I wouldn't have this on him, "It's the way Stanley would have died."

I let that pass and said, "You seem to have known him pretty well."

He turned to face me for the second time and said with chilling constraint, "Better than I would have chosen to."

I met his eyes briefly, unwillingly, then turned away to the fire again. But even then I could feel his eyes on me, pressing and prodding like I had done to him, trying to read and interpret my looks, which I tried to keep as blank as possible. I don't know whether I succeeded, but I gave it a damn hard try. But all through it the strangest thought had me in its grip, that I would hate to be a criminal brought before him when he got to be a judge, like it was already rumored he would be, if he would just consent to do a little politics or give a lot of money to one party or the other. He gave me the look of a hanging judge, long and steady and nothing held back, a look that acknowledges no tomorrow and maybe not even tonight. Then he continued, the little joke made grim by his intonation, "It goes with the territory. In my line of work you meet all kinds you'd just as soon not."

That look showed me my first mistake. I had just thought he was not the kind of man to turn himself in, but I saw now that that was by no means certain and that even he did not know what he would do when he came up the hill to me. But now he did know. He had made his judgment in the matter. In those twenty or thirty minutes, by nothing I said or done, that I know of, he had been moved to take my position, that his life was too high a price to pay for Stanley's, for what he done. But that is a position I can take only without my badge on. I know they don't balance, those two, eye for eye, and tooth for tooth. But that part of it isn't my concern. It's just my job to catch them, to detect that some wrong has been done, to find out who done it, and to prove it by the evidence. That's all. It's not my job to establish justice in the world, to know which pan of the scales you put your finger on to make things come out even; it's my job just to keep order in it. I'm just as glad. The other part, the part I'm paid to do, is hard enough. And I'm not sure there's enough money in the world to make worth wringing out your brain for a few ideas of what's fair and honest and angering most everybody else by them. There just isn't. But then there's also that old legend about Lord Nelson lifting the spyglass to his blind eye and saying truthfully enough that he saw no signal to retreat. If you do that, tho, if you take matters into your own hands like that, you have to be damn sure of what you're doing and of yourself doing it.

He could have read my mind, to say what he said next, or recognized me for the visitor in foreign parts who stops at a road sign, consults his map, and tries to figure out whether he is hopelessly lost already or on the way to being lost or in no danger at all. I had the sense that a great deal of time had passed, but nothing really had changed. The fire still burned like mad. The night air still cooled my neck. Men still moved like shadows between us and the fire. But one thing that had changed was his voice. He knew that I knew, as surely as I knew he done it. But he didn't know what I would do about it or with that knowledge any more than I did myself. And so he spoke like he meant to tease or taunt me, to call into question my ability to do anything about what he done, in the joking folksy manner of two friendly rivals talking about the same whore. Or maybe he was just scared, the way anyone would get scared. Or maybe he had split apart finally along the crack made when he and Stanley ran together for whatever reason and, in those few minutes of silence, facing the fire, had gone mad. He said sort of gaily, "They tell me you don't know what life is until you've killed a man. Has that been your experience, Sheriff? You were in Vietnam, weren't you?"

I did the best I could. "Vietnam wasn't much of a place to learn anything about life."

He kept on. "But you know what I mean."

I knew what he was aiming at but only so dimly that I couldn't recall how to counter it. "I've never heard that said before."

"But you have some idea what it means."

Again I tried to weave away from him. "Killing only teaches you about death."

Still he came on, with me beginning to feel old and sluggish like a fighter gone over the hill. "I guess you do know something about that, don't you, Sheriff? I mean, you've killed a man in the line of duty, haven't you?"

He knew as well as I did the circumstances of that shooting. But he wanted me to say it. I don't know why I obliged him. It's not something I'm particularly proud of but at the time I didn't see that I had much choice in the matter, and since then there just hasn't been anything served by trying to second-guess myself after the fact. Maybe that was reason enough to answer him, that even if I wasn't proud of it I wasn't going to let him bully me. I answered as deliberately as I could, "Yes. Once."

He seemed not to think at all, just to make casual conversation. He knew what I would say and had his next question ready. "Black man, wasn't it?"

"Yes," I said.

He corrected himself. "Or boy, wasn't it?"

I said, "He was old enough to vote. And he had a gun he knew how to use. He'd already used it."

He asked, "How did you feel when you did it? I mean, did it disturb you?"

I said, "It's not pleasant to kill a man."

He said in a voice that wasn't half there, "No, I suppose not." Then added, "But would you do it again?"

I tried not to hesitate. "I would if I had to."

He asked, "Do you think yourself a murderer?"

I was still lost in my own speculations, my own memories of the event: the pale blue light, the figure kneeling over the body and rifling its pockets, my command, the exchange of fire, all just like I was trained so I didn't even think about it at the time, and then him going down smooth and easy, taking his punishment like that, clean and quick and painless, not the interminable hell of prison. But then the jarring word, out of nowhere, not a description of the event or what I done or me, so I said without thinking, "No."

And so he carried on. "Well, what makes a murderer? Or, rather, what makes you not one?"

I gave him the party line and nothing else. "The badge does; the circumstances surrounding the use of force."

He said crisply, "Yes, of course. And you were vindicated."

He knew as well as I did what happened, but I continued to answer him. I knew what he was aiming at and wanted to see how he was going to get there. But more than that, I wanted to see what I was going to say. I'd done this before. There was the usual inquiry. But you always wonder, you wonder whether it had to be the way it turned out, something not an accident but with the marks of an accident on it. He had no right to live after what he done. But I don't know still if it was up to me to stop him like I did. Despite the chill, I felt a bead of sweat run down the length of my arm from armpit to elbow. I said sharply, "You know as well as I do. The board upheld me."

He said, "They did more than that, didn't they? They gave you a medal, didn't they?"

I corrected him. "A citation."

He slipped right around that objection. "And you deserved it. I mean, you did good work."

I repeated the line which was running through my head like a refrain, "It's not pleasant to kill a man."

He said the next thing so casual that for the first time since seeing him come up the hill toward me I doubted if he did kill Stanley. I mean, it just didn't seem that a man could be so unmoved by it. He said, "No, I expect not."

This was beginning to get to me, to make me mad, I think. I had to wonder whether I was always wrong about him. They say a man don't know himself until he faces adversity. You could say the same thing about anybody else knowing him too. Maybe he was not the man I thought. And at this moment, while he continued to press, I began to think that I could hate him and maybe already had started.

He asked, "Say, what did you do with that citation?"

I said, "It's in the office somewhere."

He said, "Oh yes. That's the one that hangs behind your desk, isn't it?"

I've never felt entirely comfortable with that constant reminder hanging over my head and that made me defensive. "The Department had it framed for me. They want us to hang up awards like that, to set a good example."

He led me along. "You do set a good example, don't you? I mean you're good at what you do."

I said, "Yes, I think I'm a good police officer."

He asked, "Do you like it?"

I paused before answering. It's a long time since anyone asked me that, the last being my wife. I said finally, "I think it's necessary to do."

He didn't have to pause. "Someone has to do it, you mean. Well, that's true enough. But why you? You're a smart man with a lot going for you. You shouldn't be bound by this necessity."

I refined my reasons, trying to remember what I said four years before to close my wife's mouth on the subject for so long. "I think it's important to do. I think you should do something you think is important."

He said quietly, "And you take pride in it, doing something important and doing it well."

I saw no reason not to admit the fact. "Yes, I do. I do take pride in it."

He concluded, "Then you must like it too, like the sense of accomplishment and so like the thing which fosters that feeling, the job itself, the demands of the job."

I wasn't ready to admit how much I did like it. "It has its unpleasant duties, like any job."

He closed on that one quick. "When most men say

that, they mean taking a foolish client out to lunch or putting up with a malicious boss."

I said simply, "My job's different."

He was beginning to feel like a swarm of bees. "Indeed. And part of it is that you are granted a special license. You're given a gun, instructed how to use it, given discretion when to use it."

I said, implying a defense, "A lot of people have guns."

He said, "But none's sanctioned to do with them what you are."

I said, "A lot of them do even so. And I'm held to account, just like anyone else."

But there he settled where he wanted to be all this time. "Not like anyone else. Held to account, perhaps, but an account rendered, any account, then showered with awards for your bravery. If you had been the one to put an end to Sims, you'd have been given another example to hang on your wall for the benefit of your men."

I didn't say anything to that, so he didn't. He'd finished what he wanted to say, had brought us to the same level, at least in his own mind, or if not that, at least made the resemblances clear. But I wasn't finished, far from it, and was just balancing on the point of asking him right out why he done it when Donnie Walsh sauntered over. I would lose nothing by it. He knew I knew or all the questions had no meaning. He had set me up and I had let him. That was all right, as far as it went. We knew where we stood now, better maybe than we ever knew before. But I didn't know why and only hesitated to ask him because I was afraid he would tell me and because I was afraid that whatever he told me would simply not be enough, either so monstrous or so mundane that I would arrest him in anger for the insult to my intelligence, the insult being that he had fooled me all these years and only made himself appear the kind of man I wanted him to be.

He was right about two things. I do know a lot about killing. I know enough to know that among the victims of violent purposeful death a good many deserve worse than they get and that it is waste of sympathy to mourn the loss of them, to feel anything for it but relief. But I'm not willing to admit that killing even those marked for death is to be done with reckless abandon and can be done at all without cost. Killing is still killing. To do it at all is to paint yourself with its colors, to place yourself always at a distance from your fellows on the earth. That's why policemen never have friends but themselves and their wives. I guess the smell of death is too strong for those who don't live with it all the time, and even we never get as used to it as you'd think. To kill is just too big. To paint yourself with it forever you've just got to have a reason equal to it, good or bad, greed or jealousy or revenge or altruism, or be mad, a raving psychopath, tho the raving might just be that one moment of consumption and all the rest the normal craziness, the isolation, of everyday life. He was also right about the relative ease with which I could get away with something just like this.

I don't know whether these two things gave him the advantage or left it with me. I had a lot else to do before getting to that and let them do the talking while I tried to imagine what would move a man of Loren's gifts and standing into such uncomfortable propensity to a man like Stanley that doing away with him by his own hand became desirable, necessary, and inevitable. It made it difficult that he was always a man to travel so much by his own lights. When his father died, he vowed never to play football again tho none of us could see any connection between those two things at all. Maybe that's what happens when you're rich. People look at you different so eventually you come to see yourself different and so unsuited to the usual way of doing things. There's no sympathy for the rich. People won't admit their troubles because they think they can just buy their way out of them and won't forgive them for having more money to do that with than the rest of us. That I would put on the debit side. On the credit side is that they can get things done faster than ordinary people, like getting their pants pressed or pushing through a petition to the city if they want something stopped or started. This is what makes Loren's crime all the more remarkable. This way, even if he was used to taking things into his own hands, just seemed to pose more risks than was necessary. And the only thing that could explain it, besides Loren being a monster or mad as hell, was that Sims done something himself so awful that Loren just needed the satisfaction of destroying him himself or that he had something so damning on Loren that the risk of doing it himself was less than the risk of public exposure.

What such a thing could be I didn't know and that had me at a disadvantage. Greed and jealousy were out, it seemed. Loren already was in the position of getting anything he wanted, more or less, simply by opening his wallet, and no woman likely to take an interest in Stanley, if there was such a woman, would make even the first appeal to a man like Loren. Altruism didn't seem to fit either, tho who did rid the world of Stanley had done the rest of us a favor. Revenge, on the other hand, was a possibility, but revenge for what. What had Stanley done to make his death necessary to balance accounts. It could've been an accident, I suppose, things gotten out of hand, but that didn't explain what they were doing together in the first place. There was a lot of explaining to do, and I had the thought suddenly that it was never going to happen. There was just too much built up between us. As much as I suspected the man, as uncomfortable as he had made me in the past, as much as I might have feared him, still I loved him too. And I owe him. I mean, what do you do with a man who gives you a record, as he done, when your own father dies, of a kind you never heard by a man you never heard of, and yet make it so right, these pieces of Ravel, with their little inscription, I found these to be a comfort in my own trouble, that you've already worn the record smooth? There's just too much. And I had only one thing to support me, if I was going to go after him at all: that I could think such a thing about him at all. If

I could I might think worse and finally work myself up to resenting him altogether and so go after him with a vengeance. No. Two things. The second being that I wanted him to be better than the rest of us as well as different than we were. I wanted the money and the looks and the power to amount to something, to do something for him. And if they didn't, I would swallow my mistake, the long mistake of fifteen years, and stop him cold.

Donnie had taken the hand Loren offered him when he walked up and then said how sorry he was about the fire, knowing, like we all did, how much his mother worked on the restoration, how sorry he and Al were they hadn't gotten there sooner, but by then there was nothing they could do and it was really only by chance they were in that neck of the woods at all, how at least, if there was anything in it for them, the man who done it got his just reward, and so on. He's a good officer, Donnie is, fair and hardworking and with enough commonness left in him, despite the party colors he wears, that ordinary people take comfort in him. He's the kind of officer I like to send to settle domestic disputes; the man, I'm afraid, I send too frequently when there is bad news to be broken. He knows those kind of things about people—frustration and grief and too little money—which often make them do things they regret, and he has sympathy for people afflicted by those ills and acts carefully but accordingly. But the county don't pay him to think any more than it pays me, and if it did it would come up short. Donnie don't think because he don't have to but also because, for all his virtues, he can't. It all ends for him with what he sees tho he sees, I guess, about as much as any man. You can't blame him. That's just the way it is. He'll work from six to six and longer like he's fighting bees if you ask him. He'll comb an acre of ground for a clue the size of a pin. I've seen him take the gun away from a man who'd already put a bullet in a fellow officer and do it with his bare hands because the street was crowded then, a feat for which the state gave him one of its local officer-of-the-year awards. I don't know anything he's afraid of and anything he don't respect. He will change his mind about things if you give him a reason to. Al, who was our first black officer, back before I joined the force, got him not to vote for Wallace in 1968, he told me, the first time he ever voted for the President, just told him not to because Wallace was a racist and not good for the country and Donnie believed him because he was black and would know a racist if he saw one, if not a man particularly good for the country. But he won't decide such things for himself. The way things are is the way they are, he says. As far as he was concerned, I could tell, we had no more work to do on this one. The county would want someone to put the blame on and a plausible theory to support the blame, and Donnie with a little luck could provide both. There was no point in going on because there was nothing more to be found. I knew different. But then I'm the kind who'll wake up nights sometimes thinking about cases we closed the book on weeks and months before, thinking why really this one or that one done what he done. Maybe I just don't know people as well as Donnie, whether they are guilty really or how much they are and what we should do about it. They tell me he don't bother to bring in a lot of them, just stops them doing what they're doing and tells them not to do it again and lets them go. And when he does bring one in, we've about one hundred percent chance of convicting him of something. He has an instinct for the difference, Donnie does. I don't. That's why I wake up, disbelieving in the teeth of the evidence that people, fully grown responsible citizens, really do the things we catch them doing. Or maybe I just can't forgive them for it. That don't make a bit of sense to Donnie. Well, you have your criminals and you have your police, he says; that's just the way it is.

He had with him an evidence bag in which I could see a pile of money, and in due course he turned it over to me, saying as he did so, "This is all we found in the car, Sheriff, at least all that don't seem to be the kind of thing anyone would have. But you don't find many cars riding around with five thousand dollars stowed under the front seat."

I didn't commit myself, taking the bag, opening it, looking in, smelling it. "Not many."

He opened up a bit, maybe for Loren's benefit, to show him how efficient we are. "Course we'll give it a better going over soon's it gets light enough to see. But I thought you prob'bly wanted to know about this right now."

I gave instructions I knew they had already followed.

"Thanks, Donnie. Just keep everybody away from the car till you can see what you're doing."

He added then, "There's one other thing, Sheriff, one thing unusual with all the rest in order."

I asked, suddenly apprehensive, "What's that?"

He gave it to me eagerly. "Well, someone smashed Sims' tape player. I mean, they didn't try to take it out and just broke it doing so. They smashed it where it was, smashed it right there and left it. Used a tire iron, it looks. We have it."

I asked before even I knew what I was after, "Any tapes?"

He smiled, approved. "I wouldn't believe it. But a good collection, in one of those fake leather carrying cases. Lot of Merle Haggard, Marty Robbins, Hank Williams, Ronnie Milsap, Waylon Jennings. Good collection, good range, old and new."

I asked in passing, "No ladies?"

He looked puzzled, trying to remember, then said, "Now you mention it, I don't recall any. Maybe I overlooked them."

I gave him more instructions. "Well, it don't matter. You just see it stays together until we get this thing finished."

He knew this was a joke and said, smiling, "Sure, Sheriff. We won't touch a thing."

That's the way it is with people, I guess. Here he was carrying around a sack of money, by his own count five thousand dollars, like it was a sack of moldy bread for his children to feed to the ducks in McClelland Park, and the thing he had his eye on was a tape or two which he could get at any discount store in town for three forty-nine plus tax each. Or maybe I don't give him enough credit and in fact what we have here is another playing out of that instinct to make discriminations, to assign weights of importance, which makes him a fine officer. He knew the money was important and would never think of tampering with it. He knew equally that the tapes probably were not important and if one or two was to slip into his pocket who was to know the difference anyway or to care. I suppose I admire that ability in a way, that quality, that ability to claim the extras of the job, that understanding of the way the world is. I've never been able to do it myself. For me everything is important. The authority against it is too strong. The way things are is not good enough. My wife for years has not asked me why I am a police officer. But she makes no end of telling me that, if I feel like that, I have no right to be one, I just can't expect any more out of people than what I get. I'm not sure she's not right and don't say anything. They've taught me that much, her and Donnie, in their own ways, at least to entertain the possibility that people were doing as good as they could already, even if it left a great deal to be desired. But Loren was different for more reasons than he was rich, and there was no reason not to expect more out of him because of it, just like as long as I've known him the normal rules of conduct have not entirely applied to him or no longer than they proved a convenience for him. That's what I meant when I said I was going to have one hell of a time proving it. You just can't tell with him, what he'd do and why. He has all the money a man can count. Very few women would have to think very long about accepting a proposition from him. You couldn't say he was exactly at peace with his community, but he did for it about what any ten other men did. There was always that about him, that he wanted somehow to do good things for the world, to make it all better, like the world was a big child with a skinned knee, to suppress the bad and promote the good. The only thing I could figure at all, given the man, was that killing Stanley was an act of retribution, a punishment for some remarkable offense, maybe even before the offense occurred. The question was what did Stanley know that none of the rest of us knew or knew anything about. My mind continued to draw blanks. I supposed it could be anything and thought how little I knew him really, how little any of us know about the rest so we can't say that, given the means, he won't do this or that. I wondered whether Loren was quite the man I thought and whether I was, whether this was not just, yes, the jealousy I had felt and the distrust of a man, however well I knew him otherwise and however little reason he had given me, a man who had that success with women. That it was, I think, which called the other images to mind. And pretty soon I found myself thinking about his sister and wondering what she had to do with this. There was always something a little strange about them, like they were too close or something, continuing to live at home and all after they were fully grown, tho you do have to wonder about Susan's age, running wild as a college girl like she does and earning her living teaching at the Episcopal kindergarten. It made a mad sort of sense that her interests were the ones which required protecting, and there are very few men, I expect, especially her brother, who would not hasten to do her bidding. In her own sweet way, she is the most crazily wasteful woman I've ever known and surely capable of getting herself involved in some hairbrained scheme which she would naturally expect her brother to get her out of. In this I began to see a certain promise and to feel a certain satisfaction. But what I needed was simply some more information. I warmed up to the effort, breaking into the silence they had let fall over us. "What would you say this money does to your theory, Loren?"

He answered slowly, in true lawyerly fashion. "Perhaps something, perhaps nothing. It was only a theory."

I pressed him on it. "I mean it just don't seem reasonable for a conspirator to abandon such a tidy sum."

He said, "Maybe the conspirator didn't know it was there. Maybe he knew it was there, but knew there was something wrong with it, so that it was useless to him."

I completed it for him. "Like it was counterfeit."

He said only, "It's possible."

I prodded, "You're just full of theories. You want to tell me about the tape player."

He said, "Maybe the incidents aren't related."

I considered this for a moment more seriously than

I meant to. "No. That gets too complicated. Either there was none or there was one. At least for the time being."

Just then the time being got put off a bit. A station wagon came lumbering to a stop beside us. Unlike everyone else, the driver, a skinny young fellow with long blond hair, had not stopped with the other cars down the hill but had pushed his right up the yard in front of the church. And the first thing I said to him as he got out was why didn't he go ahead and take that vehicle and put it down below where it belonged.

He spoke in a voice very close to a whine, enough itself to make me run him off. "But Sheriff, I got a lot of equipment here."

I gave him my opinion on that and a shortened version of my instruction, and Donnie, like he always does, shifted slightly so he was in the driver's better view and rested his hand on the butt of his gun. "You'll manage. Take it back down."

By that time, his associate had removed himself from the other side of the car and come around to greet us. I knew him well and hated him to the bones, a fact he knew and emphasized now by taking my side of it. "The Sheriff's right, Jimmy. The car might get in the way up here. You better go ahead and do what he says."

As if that wasn't enough, he then added, smiling with all the sincerity of a politician, "Besides, we got to learn to support our local police."

He turned to us without waiting for an answer and so did not see Jimmy silently hoist his middle finger in salute. Smiling, always smiling, he said, "Good evening, gentlemen. Or I guess at this hour I should say, good morning."

I could not resist sowing a little dissent where I could, where I knew it would grow like wildfire. I ignored the greeting, looked passed the man, said sternly to the boy, who apparently did not care that we saw what he done: "I'm going to trust that you had something else in mind than that, son, and just got confused."

To my surprise and amusement, he said, "No, Sheriff, I know what I done and Sid does too."

Sid, whose smile by this time had collapsed and hardened in place like an overdone cake, was Sidney Mueller, star investigative reporter for W-LEX TV, only investigative reporter and a star only in comparison to nothing else, a flashlight poking under people's beds in the vast darkness of the universe. He was a man, in my opinion, of no moral fiber whatsoever, a bundle of beatitudes and half-truths held together by the single powerful urge to make it in the world. But then my opinion is biased. For Sidney had made the occasion of my killing that black man the opportunity for discovering his own black blood, a fact he had spent every day since he was twelve attempting to deny, and tried, on the basis of those two happenstances, to establish his credentials as a reporter and a great human being. His careful hints about some kind of wrongdoing on the air succeeded only in drawing out a crowd of indignant black citizens to picket our office and demand my trial for homicide. They got the usual inquest, which scarcely satisfied them, tho Al, for political reasons and with no precedent, sat on the board as an ex-official member. Nothing else came of it, except the citation. He remained with us, cockier and more certain of himself than ever. I don't in general mind cockiness in people, so long as they have some claim to it, like the high school football team after a victory, and that's not what I hate him for, after the purely impartial hatred I have for him because of his disregard for the truth. What I hate is that attitude, that sense he has that he is somehow the offended party. He genuinely believed there was nothing personal in the attack. Until the incident, I think he liked me fine, by his own lights at least; and after it he felt only disappointment that I wasn't big enough news to hoist him up in the world. Since that time I've noticed a real condescension in his dealings with me. No sympathy, just the clucking poorfool attitude of one himself beyond reproach or infection. That's reason enough to hate a man, no need for all the rest, him looking down his nose at you to save himself the trouble of looking you in the eye. Yes. I did hate him, no prejudice intended, with no urge first to explain anything. We just had different systems at heart and that was the end of it. I guess someone told him that both regard for the truth and sympathy would just weigh him down on his rise to the top. Or maybe he was just smarter than I thought and figured it out for himself. In any case he got rid of both real early. He had everything else too to make his way easier. He dressed good, as good as Loren and in many of the same clothes, like he paid someone in Walden's to dress him exactly like their best young customer. Finely cut suits, silk shirts, dainty little shoes from Italy—he must have spent a fortune on that look. But I had to admit he had the body for the clothes and the face. They say he played college ball down in Orangeburg until he got hit once too often by those hungry dudes trying to impress the pro scouts and decided to hang it up, claiming an injury that never healed properly, and transferred to the university and began to take courses in TV, where he could take advantage of those looks and that subdued color, only a shade or two darker than the camel hair coat he wore. The firelight turned his hair to the color of copper wire. His teeth gleamed while he spoke. I caught myself thinking idly under what circumstances I would kill him and being immediately grateful that thought comes very cheap.

Smiling, accommodating, he was trying to pump information out of us even before Jimmy got the equipment out—how did it start, did we suspect arson— each of which I evaded, when I had to, claiming the ongoing investigation, anything hollowly official to keep him away from me. I was doing it all from memory, scarcely listening to his questions and not listening at all to what the others said when he grew tired of badgering me and let them have the benefit of one of his comments. I had so much to think about before I had any chance of knowing what kind of evidence I would need. I did detect the movement, however, but not in time to stop it, tho I don't know that I would have in any case because I genuinely enjoyed the look of surprise and fear which twisted Sidney's face when Loren grabbed him by the lapels and jerked their faces close together. Now Sidney's about my size, a good five inches taller than Loren and forty pounds or so heavier, and in order to get their faces close enough together for whatever he had to say, Loren had to haul himself up on that chest which, when Sidney drew back with a grimace, puffed itself up like a turkey's. It was truly comic, despite their expressions, and I worked hard not to laugh as Donnie and I worked to separate them, saying, "Now wait a minute there, boys. Just slow down. Now, what's going on here?"

Loren was grim, his jaw worked hard, and the words came out like coarse meal. "You heard it, Sheriff."

Sidney was indignant, now that he was no longer scared, and smoothed his lapels with exaggerated care and also called me to bear witness. "You saw it, Sheriff."

I spoke to him first. "You don't look hurt. Now just settle down."

He exclaimed, "We'll see about that! We'll see who's hurt and who's going to be! You got that, Jimmy?"

Jimmy answered from a short distance away, "Got what, Sid?"

Sid turned his anger on Jimmy. "Goddam it! Don't you have that thing working yet? This man attacked me, and I want a record of it. I'm not going to let him get away with it."

Jimmy played it dumb as could be and I could have kissed him. "Gee, sorry, Sid. I got nothing."

He paused for some moments before answering and during that time turned his indignant look on each of us in turn, which neither Donnie nor I were buying and which Loren didn't connect with. And when he spoke again, he addressed his words to Jimmy without looking at him and the tone was full of ice. "Don't call me Sid. The name is Sidney. Anyway, you saw what happened. That's enough."

Jimmy didn't hesitate. "Saw what, Sid? Sidney."

I'll say this for the man, he knew when he was beat. He took a few moments more to gather himself together, to cast a cold stare around again, then went off to find a better angle to shoot the fire from, a spot to show him to best advantage, with Jimmy laboring along behind with his equipment and, I saw for the first time, a young woman no older than Jimmy bringing up the rear and carrying what I took to be more equipment. At that moment I would almost have felt sorry for him if there hadn't been so much already to make that impossible. I had not misjudged the man, I knew; he was like I described him. But I failed by that to take into account all those factors mitigating against him turning out to be a decent, tolerant, respectful sort of man. I would not forgive him for not being that despite the odds. But when they were out of hearing and I sought an explanation, I noticed a sharper tone in my voice than I intended. "Now just what the hell is the matter with you? What is going on here?"

He repeated what he said. "You heard it."

I played the cop and spoke the truth. "I heard nothing."

His defense sounded crazy. "Then that's what you were meant to hear."

I tried to be reasonable myself. "Now listen, Loren.

The man is going to make trouble and I just want to know what's going on."

He said back, not listening or thinking or caring, "Trouble for you perhaps, but not for me. The man can't even spell his own name unless you give him two tries."

I was stumped. "What does that have to do with it?"

He murmured, "He just doesn't know enough to sue."

I got pretty heated at this point. "He don't have to know more than to know you mussed his fine coat. That's all he has to know. The rest he'll leave to some-one else."

He said, "We'll see."

I let it get out of hand then. " 'We'll see,' hell. That's exactly what I don't want to do. I want to see now. I don't want one of my own men serving me with a subpoena next week when I don't even know what happened."

He said, as cool as you please, "That's your prob-lem, Sheriff."

This was maddening and I let him know it. "I ought to arrest you right now and let you spend the rest of the morning in jail thinking about my problem."

He answered me slowly and at first I thought he was giving up. "Maybe you ought to do that. I think you'll find my fees are reasonable."

I was aware suddenly that I was making more out of this than it deserved and thought I knew why. But I kept on anyway, having to do something to settle myself down, and turned to Donnie. "Donnie, what the hell is going on here?"

He looked genuinely confused himself and said, "I'm damned if I know, Sheriff. Sid was just standing there, smiling like a cheddar cat, and suddenly Loren went after him."

I said, "Well, he must have said something. You just don't jump a man for sport."

Donnie's confusion made his voice rise. "I swear I didn't hear a thing. Just normal talk, you know. Sid just running off at the mouth, as usual, such a sad thing and all and won't the town miss it and won't his mother miss it. Just talk and nothing else, I swear."

I said, "All right, all right. If that's the way it is, that's the way it is. I know nothing, saw nothing, heard nothing. It was a fragment of my imagination. I'm free of it altogether."

Loren said, as cold and grim as ever but still able to give it more than any normal person would, "Fine, Sheriff. I'm glad to see you've finally become a man of reason."

I shot back, "Well, I'll say this. If that's the case, I'm glad it don't take one to know one."

He conceded, "All right. Let's just leave it at that then. I'm crazy, I'm hearing voices. If he presses charges you'll have to bear witness to my temporary insanity."

I gave it a last try. "Well, that's what I want to know. What did those voices of yours say?"

But he had enough and pretended complete innocence tho he murmured his question and turned to stare at the fire, which is not what an innocent man would do. "What voices, Sheriff?"

That was it; I had enough too. I threw up my hands and let them fall limply to my sides. "Oh hell, I give up. If it's that important to you, go on to jail, for all I care. I've got more to think about than why a couple of full-grown men see fit to push each other around like boys in a sandbox."

On the other hand, I knew, that's exactly what I did have to think about, why two grown men didn't act like it, but instead like their undeveloped parts, if I was going to do anything at all. There's always the temptation in this job to let the explanations go. You give the court what it wants. You collect your evidence, establish your motives and opportunities, call your alibis into question, point your finger squarely at the man you think done it. But explanations are not called for, the whole skein of what the psychologists call the situational and dispositional factors. They take too much time, which is bad enough, but worse than that, they just confuse the issue. Too many of the murders we try would be found to be justified if we went too far into them. So we say, no, there was a crime by our lights, and you done it and you'll be punished for it, and that's an end of it; next case. It don't work well maybe, but it works. And there's a whole lot more guilty ones running free, let me tell you, than innocent ones behind bars, a whole lot more. We don't catch them all, by a long shot. Some of them are too smart, have done the job too well, profited by the normal share of fool's luck. It's just a lot easier to get away with a crime than most people think, and those who get caught have usually got scared and made some mistake. But we try, beating our heads against the wall until we see the crack in it or our heads, working on it until the public ruckus has subsided and, if the stakes are small enough, we can stow the file in the back of the cabinet. There's new ones always coming along. That's one thing about this job. You never hurt for business. That's what makes a case like this so hard to get worked up over. There's just too much else to do. And unless there's something really amiss, like Loren stove in Sims' head with that tire iron he used to break the tape deck or something else to make him lay down like that and play dead until he could set a fire around him and do it in earnest, it will be hard not to go ahead and close the book on this one. No theory of ours has ever taken account of all the facts, but those odd ones we just ignore. Donnie and Al'll be pleased. We'll have had an easy night of it. A little lost sleep is all. Fate's done us a favor we couldn't do for ourselves. The newspapers will love it. Suspected vandal sets torch to self. We'll see a certain justice in that. The man got what he deserved. There's no use breaking our heads against the wall for nothing.

The only one not served by it being no explanation would be myself, and I wasn't sure that my claim on things was so great that I couldn't do without. That didn't mean that I didn't want to know any less, but just that I didn't know if I was entitled, any more than anyone else. Me being sheriff didn't make it any easier because I knew I wanted to know for other reasons than a sheriff's. Or I wanted to know as ordinary citizen first, just me and him, before I had to do that. But I was getting nothing from him now. The clean straight lines and planes of his face were grim and unyielding as stone. I studied him as best I could out of the corner of my eye, but it would take a lot more insight than I had to see inside and a lot more time and effort than I could spare to wear him down from the outside. I have never felt so torn between things in my life. I stood my ground but felt at any moment I was going to break apart and everything in me come spilling out. I was trying to decide what was fair, I was trying to count what I owed him for being my friend and for not trusting him, I even thought I might just do it, do it without question, haul him in and book him and pass the blame along to my boss or the society or justice in the abstract which I pledged to serve when I put the badge on. It wasn't my fault, I didn't tell him to go out and do it, to flaunt the law like that. Then I would lose my way again and wander off into another part of the woods, wander off, then wander back, and come again upon the stubborn and unmovable fact that a crime had been committed and that meant a punishment was due. It was simple. It was also not so simple. For not to punish the crime when I knew it and the per- petrator knew I knew it was to tolerate it, and to tolerate it was to approve it, and to approve it was to encourage it. To tolerate it was to tolerate it easier next time. I do not make these distinctions well. I felt at any moment I would split apart. I was not sure that Stanley, having broken laws with reckless abandon, deserved the pro-

tection of the law. No. I was sure he didn't. He sur-
rendered that right. He deserved his punishment. But
here was what I didn't understand. Just because he
didn't deserve the protection, that didn't mean that the
one who did the crime against him didn't deserve his
punishment. All these cases have three parties—the
two beating on each other and the society—and the
last one is the most anxious and demanding to see its
interests served. I was hired to see that done for them,
and that made it simple. But it made it hard again that
no one really cared about what they didn't know, and
but for me no one ever would know, and that brought
it down to me and him again, and that made it important after all that there was an explanation, something, something to warrant taking a man's life for it,
even a life as twisted and ugly as Stanley Sims'.

The fire had died some, but not enough to get
the body out and not so much that I couldn't see his
face clearly out of the corner of my eye, a face like a
bronze mask. For the most part the firemen were just
standing around. There was not a whole lot they could
do, and they were mostly concerned to see that the
fire didn't spread to the woods beyond and burn up
the paper company's trees. They shifted around, silhouettes against the bright orange blaze. Maybe it was
the hour or my own fatigue, but I found something
dreamlike in their slow purposeless movements, the
movements of men with nothing to do but wait, something beautiful, something reassuring. The fire was contained at least. That was the best they could do and
the best we could hope for. It was not their fault the

fire started, nor that they were so late to be called, nor that the building was so far from water, nor that it was set to burn like a charm. They were just volunteers after all and were paid less to be heroes than we were to think. But they had come and they were there now, and the television people had come and now gone, which somehow made the event more dreamlike and more real. Shortly the coroner showed up when we finally managed to convince him that someone needed his services and he convinced himself that the poor stiff had waited long enough. I was exhausted by my own struggle, that tension required to hold everything together, that on top of the usual day of thefts and altercations and complaints on one side that we were inefficient and on the other that we were corrupt and abusive. I kept wondering why I did it at all. Even the cold wasn't helping anymore. I wanted badly my long hot bath and my wife to pour me out a stiff drink and sit on the edge of the tub, still half-asleep but just in case I needed to get something off my chest, which she would only half listen to but then would surprise me with a day or two from now by asking me about, why this or that. She'd solved cases for me like that before, calling to mind things I forgot or failed to consider carefully. Maybe that was what I needed, that and sleep and the time for something unforeseen to turn up or the time for all these things to settle into their natural place after I'd taken the stick to them so and stirred them up. It was going to be damn hard, I knew, to do anything more myself without raising more questions from the wrong people than I was prepared to answer. We had a lock on the case. It would raise eyebrows all around for me to go asking any questions except the routine ones I had to ask Sims' family. They weren't likely to make any connection for me at all. I knew their type before I even met them, having grown up among them, suspicious already of the police, who don't protect them but stop them from speeding or roust them for getting drunk and fighting, tho almost all of us come right from them and still live among them. They weren't likely to know any of his activities or associates. I had to ask, but I didn't expect to learn anything. And that would pretty much end it. Unless something unexpected turned up. Unless the loose ends became too obvious and we couldn't just leave them lay. Unless the puzzle when we put it together had too many holes even for us. I couldn't go asking Loren's secretary. Hardly that old dragon. He always complains about how nosy she is. But he knows and I know from having tried it before that she stands watch over his interests with the silent, steadfast, and un- questioning devotion of a mother tiger over her cubs. I couldn't get anything out of her if I tried for ten years. I couldn't go asking his mother. I had no grounds, nothing to say. Did you know Sims? Did Loren? Did you know Loren killed him? Do you know why? No. His mother would say that, if Loren did do it, he must have had a good reason. Nor his sister, despite my theory that she's the connection. Drugs maybe, or just the kicks, the wild unconcern of her own and the con- tempt for that life everyone else wants and she has and continues to live. She's just crazy enough to be tied up with a man like Sims, crazy and wild and just as sweet to be with as honey. That would fit, that would put the pieces all together, what I know of her, what I know of him. He did it to protect her, to get revenge for her. He's always had this thing about her anyway, would think no ill of her, would tolerate no suggestion. There was that time he took two of them out into the parking lot behind the Capri Lounge at the same time, going to make them both take it back at the same time, and Lord, he was already well into it by the time I got there. Lord, when was that? Six or seven years ago. I was still in a patrol car in town. He must have been about the first year of law school. Blood all over his shirt, the ring around them silent as a bunch of monks. They said those two were a little too drunk and making bets a little too loud on how many she could take in one night. It was something a brother had to do something about. You can't let people talk about your sister like that. But even so, he wouldn't face the fact of what she is, however she got there. Even I know that. Even I had my chance with her. But I blew it, I guess you'd say. She's so pretty and she said the thing so fast and loose and sweet that by the time I got it all figured out she'd already smiled and departed. Loren just can't face that, the way she is. But that's always been his way. And I honestly don't think I can blame him for it. Except that the result this time was not a black eye or a broken bone but a corpse.

I won't even try to tell the time between when the television people took their pictures and left and Loren said that the problem with Sidney was that there was no place in our town where he might be seen as he saw himself and when he said what he said next, taking me by surprise with it and leaving me as far behind as ever. It was a long time, I know that. Donnie had long since shuffled off to find what else he could in the dark. I was almost asleep on my feet, having pretty much decided that I was going to just have to wait and see. I was so tired in fact that it was not until he spoke that I saw he had been watching me for some time. "What you think you know, you don't."

I felt I had only half a brain to work on that one and to do everything else I had to do as well, to turn my head to face him and to say something to keep him talking. It felt like hours before I could get the words out. "Suppose you tell me about it."

Either he was as tired as I was or my ears were working as slow as my tongue because it was an equally long time before I heard him. "A man's dead. Burned alive."

That he seemed to be as bad off as I was made me bold, made me speak hastily. "I can see what happened. I want to know why."

I saw then my mistake. He was not as tired as I was, he had not weakened, he drew still on some incredible reserve that no other man of my acquaintance has ever had access to. I have seen men face their own deaths and the deaths of buddies and loved ones. I've seen some lose their minds and others gain a measure of strength from the adversity itself. I have known men to weep, to laugh, to show fear, to show determination, to show nothing. I have known those same emotions mold my face in those same ways against my will. But I have never known a face do what his done. That stern unyielding look of stone and down one side of it like a scar the track of a tear. His eyelids did not blink; his eyes did not quaver. He fixed me with a stare to teach me my own ways with those accused into whose actions I've inquired. But I know that trick and it was not what broke me. That tear broke me. That evidence contradicting everything else. That second idea. That he could feel both remorse and no repentance. I knew that till then I could do pretty much what he done and been pretty much like him, as brave, as strong. But I could not have done that tear. I could not have done both things. And it broke me to realize it. All I could do then was repeat, "I want to know why, Loren."

He turned his face to the fire like he didn't want to embarrass me, like I made some terrible mistake, and didn't say anything for a long time. He looked at the fire and then he said, "I'd better go give my mother the bad news."

I didn't turn, but I could hear the crackling of the dead leaves as he walked away and the slam of the car door and the rumble of the little sports car he drives. In front of me, the flames burned down, and the firemen kept watch over it like over a young crop they were afraid a late frost would get. We were a long time waiting for the end. It was well after dawn, a good hour of the day gone, before we could get Sims' earthly remains out from among the ashes and the charred timbers of the old church. It was Sims we learned later that day. Just then we only supposed it was, with some additional but mysterious reason. The corpse clutched in one charred hand a tape cassette, now black and twisted and unidentifiable. In the other odd facts of Sims' life this seemed a very small and unimportant one. It just don't seem to matter whose voice of his collection he chose to take with him to his grave.

That was it. Donnie walked back down the hill with me and leaned on the door of my car as I inserted the ignition key. He had something on his mind which he finally gave voice to. "Don't Loren look broke up about this? I mean, he looks to me like his insides was all sucked out."

I turned on the car and said with little apparent concern, "I didn't notice."

He backed off a step, shrugged, "Well, maybe I was mistaken. Maybe it was just the light."

I said, "Maybe so."

That night on the news, Sidney Mueller posed a few unspecific questions about the peculiar circumstances of the fire and death, but this time there was no demonstration and no inquest. It's my story and his. We alone share the terrible secret, and this is my part of it. They tell me the tape will last a long time. But I don't know what for. A record of my doing and his. I won't tell my wife about this one. There's some things even a wife shouldn't have to know. But there it will be anyway. The secret. Our secret. The great temptation.